Hunger

Hunger

Mohamed El-Bisatie

Translated by
Denys Johnson-Davies

The American University in Cairo Press
Cairo   New York

This paperback edition published in 2014 by
The American University in Cairo Press
113 Sharia Kasr el Aini, Cairo, Egypt
420 Fifth Avenue, New York, NY 10018
www.aucpress.com

Exclusive distribution outside Egypt and North America by I.B.Tauris & Co Ltd.,
6 Salem Road, London, W2 4BU

Dar el Kutub No. 10467/14
ISBN 978 977 416 680 8

Dar el Kutub Cataloging-in-Publication Data

El-Bisatie, Mohamed
        Hunger / Mohamed El-Bisatie.—Cairo: The American University in
    Cairo Press, 2014
        p.   cm.
        ISBN 978 977 416 680 8
        1. English fiction
        823

1 2 3 4 5   18 17 16 15 14

Designed by Andrea El-Akshar
Printed in Egypt

*T*he front of the house was built of red bricks. The bottom of it had swelled up through damp and some of the bricks had fallen away. Large gaps had been patched up with cement. The door was of thick wood and above it, on the wall, had been written with a brush in white letters: *Enter it in Peace and Safety.*

The color was still bright and the words, despite the many years they had been there, were still complete. The small boy in the house used to take care of them: though he himself couldn't read or write he liked the shape of them, and ever since his eyes had opened onto the world he had seen them whenever he was about to enter the house. He would climb up the door to clean the letters of dust and wash them down with a wet rag.

The side and inner walls of the house were of mud. The sole room was roofed over with wooden beams, while half the courtyard was unroofed, allowing the light to enter day and night; the other half had a trellis composed of a mixture of tree branches, palm fronds, strips of tin, and old rags that hung down and did not look greatly different from the snakes that squirmed alongside them.

The stone bench occupied a deep hollow that was like a cave in front of the door. It was large enough for the family to sleep on it head to tail when it was too hot.

The Husband

As usual when there is no bread left in the house, Sakeena wakes up early and seats herself on the stone bench, with her headcloth rolled up in her lap, having washed her face and put on the one gallabiya that she possesses and that she has had for many years; it has grown thin with time, and the color of its roses has disappeared. She does not sleep in it, making do with her shift, with its many patches.

She is joined by her husband and the two boys, who are still sleepy. One of them is twelve, and the younger one—Ragab—nine. This one throws himself down with his head on her thigh and goes off to sleep. The older boy, Zahir, squats down beside the door frame, her husband on the other end of the bench, cleaning his teeth with a piece of straw.

She mutters in an inaudible whisper, "So, he cleans them. He eats filth and cleans them."

But she realizes what he is driving at by cleaning his teeth: he is hungry and is reminding her to hurry up and look around for something that will assuage his hunger. The four of them went to sleep with empty stomachs; their sleep was disrupted. She felt the two boys sitting up during their sleep, looking around here and there, then lying down again. But what could she do? Her husband had spent the last money he had two days ago—he bought a cigarette, though he did not smoke.

"But there you are, that's what happened."

He returned at night with the lighted cigarette between his lips.

When he saw her and the two boys piled up on the stone bench, he pressed the lighted end of the cigarette between his fingers and shoved it into his pocket.

As always, she was seated on the stone bench waiting for daybreak so that she could call at the houses of the women she knew to borrow a couple of loaves of bread. Sometimes she was successful, sometimes not. She would always give back what she borrowed—she might be late in doing so but she always gave it back. She would not wait until they asked her. Occasionally she would come across one of the women, who would not say anything, though her face spoke the words, and Sakeena would tell her, "It's all right—I'll be baking in a couple of days." The woman's face would remain unchanged, as though Sakeena had said nothing.

But baking day showed no signs of coming. Her husband did not shift from his dormant state: he worked for a couple of days and was idle for ten. The things she wanted to say to him she would mumble to herself. After all, every man in the quarter worked, and there was not a child at home hungry or naked, but he did not care. Night and day he lay in the reception room or sat on the bench or loafed around the souk. He loafed around the whole night, sitting with the men who sat on the benches or in the small mosques, or standing with those who stood around not doing a damn thing, laughing with whoever laughed, nodding his head in agreement when he saw them agreeing with something that had been said, choosing to go with the majority, and following them until they dispersed, then going back to look for others.

"And what is it you like so much about all that, Zaghloul?" she asks herself.

She had learned all about his nature: no sooner did she see him stretch out on the bench with his hands in the openings in the sides of his gallabiya, feeling his stomach, looking right and left, than she knew that he was fed up with sitting down and wanted to see what was going on in the world, and that he would not be returning before day-break, after the cafés were all closed, along with the souk street that he liked better than all others, where every sort and kind of person congregated and where there were many lights and shops.

"His new mood's become worse with the business of pay-ing condolences," she tells herself.

There was not a condolence gathering in the village without him seeking it out. He would walk off to it wher-ever it was and stay in the marquee that had been set up until the Quran reader finished his recitation, and then he would help with clearing up the chairs. When the mar-quee workers saw him so enthusiastic, they let him get on with the job of collecting the chairs and stacking them up on the two carts, leaving them free to take down the marquee. He never tired: despite how thin and emaciated he looked, his bones were strong and firm. Once she saw him carry a four-doored wardrobe on his back, taking it from a cart of wedding furnishings to a neighboring bridal home.

"Oh, what a day—and people don't forget."

A couple of years before—the same street and also a bride's wedding furnishings.

"Samia the daughter of Khalil—and who'll forget her?"

The wardrobe was on top of the cart, held by two men on each side, its large mirror shining and bringing everything into view, even the women on the roofs, more than one of whom were squatting down, oblivious of the fact that they were showing their legs in fleeting snatches in the mirror, though their heads did not appear.

"Cover yourselves, you up there on the roof!" came a shout.

The boys clung onto the cart, craning to see and bursting into shouts at what the mirror revealed.

"Oh, what a day it was!"

The lane was narrow where the bridegroom had his house, so the cart could not get in. They brought it to a stop at the top of the lane and the four men lowered the wardrobe off the cart and walked with it into the lane. They were bent over, their faces against the wardrobe, their gallabiyas tucked up and knotted around their waists, moving their feet gingerly, the veins standing out on their foreheads.

"God be praised—What wonders He can perform!"

When the knot in one of the men's gallabiyas came loose, he tripped over its hem and fell on his back. The other three were thrown off balance and the whole thing came down like a house falling, scattering into eight different pieces here and there. Not a single inch of the mirror escaped intact: splinters of it reached deep into the lane, and the trilling cries of joy turned to shrieks, wailing, and the slapping of faces in grief.

"Oh, what a thing to happen on the wedding night—a bad omen."

That's how it was.

The groom did not utter a word. He came running and cast a glance at the scattered wardrobe and went back home. They followed him with the rest of the furniture. The festivities were completed—trilling cries of joy and tearful eyes—with everyone expecting some disaster but not knowing where it would come from.

The groom went in to consummate the marriage, the bride having bathed and plaited her hair.

The following day he returned her to her father's house.

Khalil, the bride's father, had bought half his daughter's furniture on credit.

"God willing, at the time of the cotton," he told the owner of the furniture store.

There were another seven months before the cotton crop would be ready, but the owner of the store agreed and took promisory notes from Khalil. However, the cotton that had been planted would not suffice. He said, "When it comes time to pay, the good Lord will solve that. The important thing is not to expose the girl to scandal."

And the girl went back to her father's house.

"And those who had something to say said it."

There was a lot of talk: a bride going back to her father's house a day after her marriage?

"No, there's something wrong."

Khalil—perhaps the whisperings did not reach him, or otherwise he would have behaved differently, God alone knows—said, "I'll buy another wardrobe and be done with it."

And there would never be enough cotton.

He took himself off to the house of Khalifa the groom.

"I'll take him with me," he said. "He can choose whichever one he likes."

Khalifa met him with head lowered and a dejected look.

"I don't want a wardrobe, or anything else."

Khalifa was a man who knew God. He had learned the Quran by heart and sometimes gave judgments about religious matters, and would permit certain people to kiss his hand as he mumbled, "God forgive me." And when he passed a place for prostration at prayer time he would make the call and lead the prayer, but he never tried to lead the people in prayer at the mosque, where there were sheikhs capable of stopping him.

Khalil did not understand. He looked at Khalifa in confusion, his hands clenched in his lap. "And all that anger of yours? That's the way things happened. It was a matter of fate."

Khalifa became very worked up. "Yes, you've said it—a matter of fate. Whenever anything happens, you people say that."

Khalil's bewilderment increased; he glanced around him and looked at the open door of the room. "By God, I don't understand a thing: a cupboard got broken, so we'll get another one."

Khalifa was still upset. "You don't understand?"

"By God, son, I don't understand."

Then all of a sudden it occurred to him what had caused him to doubt things. He froze where he was as he mumbled, "Tell me, Khalifa, did you sleep with the girl?"

"Of course I slept with her."

"And the girl was intact?"

"God forgive me, you're not thinking properly."

"Thank God."

He was silent as with his finger he removed some of the drops of sweat that had collected on his face. "So what's wrong?" he asked.

"Uncle Khalil, O Uncle Khalil, what happened was a message. If the wardrobe had fallen far from here, we wouldn't have said much, but a couple of steps away from the house—and on the wedding day—what can you make of that, Uncle Khalil? This was a sign that said, Look out."

"Look out for what?"

"Look out for this marriage—it's not right, there's something wrong with it. It may show itself today, tomorrow, or after a year, but it's there."

"And if that's what was in your mind, why did you sleep with the girl?"

"I wanted to know, Uncle Khalil, I wanted to know whether the fault was in her. In short, just as we went in on friendly terms, let's leave on friendly terms. We're at your disposal for anything you want."

So they left on friendly terms.

For a week or two the whisperings did not stop—people

couldn't believe this had happened. They knew that Khalifa saw omens in things, yet he was also a man of virtue, and perhaps he had wanted to protect the girl, having discovered she was not a virgin. So he had said what he said and sent her on her way.

The girl herself was perplexed by the looks people gave her. She did not go out at all. Those women who entered the house would avoid looking at her or talking to her. But when she stood at the front door, she sensed that the eyes of any woman who happened to be passing by enveloped her from top to bottom, her mouth askew.

The girl's mother, because of all the talk she had heard, had her doubts about her. The girl was her daughter and she knew every step she had taken, but even so she told herself, "What a disaster! What if it's true?"

She locked the girl and herself alone in the room and turned to her, her face sullen and her eyes ablaze. "Now tell me about the talk I've been hearing this last week."

The girl had no idea what it was about. She believed what Khalifa had told her father. "What talk?" she answered her mother.

The mother began, and she said this and she said that and the girl could only listen. The blood drained from her face and her trembling legs could not hold her, and she collapsed.

She did not get up again. She lasted a day and a night then passed away.

The days went by and there was another wedding ceremony in the same street, and the lane—a couple of lanes away from Khalifa's house—was too narrow, and the four men who were holding onto the wardrobe on the cart refused to carry it to the groom's house. They remembered what had happened before. From the moment they entered the lane each of them thought about it, and some of them whispered, "God have mercy on her—she died a pointless death."

There was a crush in the street and around the corners of the alleys. They were waiting, and the cart stood at the head of the lane where the groom's house was. He was standing in front of the open door waiting for them, while the four men on the cart were in two minds. The bride's relatives were talking to them, while others had joined in, and the four men were staring at them from on top of the cart, silent and motionless.

Zaghloul appeared from nowhere. He saw and heard what was going on and he took off his gallabiya and threw it to someone. Spotting him, Sakeena rushed to get to him, wanting to remind him about the tear in the seat of his underpants alongside his emaciated buttocks. Some of the bystanders hid their smiles, at which Sakeena moved off abashed.

Zaghloul went up to the cart and talked with the four men. Turning to him, they weighed him up with their eyes. Perhaps among all the people they were the ones who knew what he was capable of.

They turned the wardrobe around and cautiously inclined it until it was resting on Zaghloul's back. They then walked along on either side of the wardrobe with their hands ready to grasp hold of it.

Everyone else walked behind him until the whole lane was packed with people, all expecting what had happened before to be repeated.

It was as though the wardrobe was moving along on its own. Zaghloul was concealed underneath it, nothing of him showing. At one moment Sakeena got a glimpse of his feet slowly advancing. Then she saw his legs with their protruding veins almost bursting out from his skin. At one time he came to a stop and everyone held their breath, thinking that the moment had come. The four men adjusted the position of the wardrobe slightly.

Eventually he arrived, and the wardrobe entered the house. The lane resounded to trilling cries of joy, but there was no sign of Zaghloul. She turned around here and there, but could not see him. Then she saw him beside her, dusting down his gallabiya.

"What are you doing here?" he asked her.

"I saw you."

She was on the stone bench, glancing at him sideways. He was cleaning his teeth with the straw.

"What is it, Sakeena?" she said to herself. "So many things to think about."

He did not look tired, not until he reached home. Then it was, "Oh my back, my side. All right—at any rate, thanks be to God."

As she rubbed his back she asked him, "So what about the condolence session, and carrying the chairs?"

"Yes, that bit." It was the middle of his back, and he was groaning, "Go easy."

Her hand came and went along his spine. She asked him the same question again, and he replied, "Yes, it was the condolence session, and they were shifting chairs. What of it?"

"And so you were paid something?"

"Not at all—one gets one's reward from God, woman."

"Reward? You mean to say you didn't get anything?"

"What 'anything,' woman? It's God's reward, I'm telling you."

"And your children also get that reward?"

"My children? What have my children got to do with it, you silly bitch?"

Roughly brushing her hand away from his back, he sat up. Though she had never been beaten by him, his moments of anger frightened her: his eyes would look as though they saw nothing in front of him. He would immediately be in a bad mood if she talked to him about their pitiful state.

As soon as he had had his fill of being lazy and loafing about, he would look around for work. He was good at anything: making coffee, tinning copper, portering, building work, panel-beating. He would not look around for long but would accept the first job that came his way. He would do the work of three men. In the café he would do two shifts one after the other: he would clean the place in the early hours after the late night's work, and he would sleep there, just two hours, and then the owner would wake him before daybreak. "What's with you, Zaghloul— still sleeping?"

She would not see him on the days he was working. He sent her a young lad employed in the café to give her the money and ask her for a clean change of clothes. Anybody hearing the boy talk would think Zaghloul had five or more changes of clothes, but there was just the one, and she could not remember whether she had washed it. There been no soap in the house since the last time he had worked. Perhaps as usual she had simply rinsed the clothes through with water to get rid of the dirt and mud.

Her hand closed over the money, overcome with joy. For a long time no money had entered her pocket nor had she even touched it. Turning her back on the boy and before counting it up, she moved her head and noticed that the boy was still there. She eyed him in surprise. "What are you standing there for?"

"The clothes."

"What clothes?"

The change of clothes for her husband. She had forgotten. She hesitated. She had not been able to count the money. She would do it when she went into the house to bring the change of clothes.

The baking. She would do it today, right away. There would be two piasters left over. A little sugar and tea. And a round of cheese. No, half a round would be plenty. A dish of molasses, and maybe a bit of rice and lentils. Or what about rice and forget about the lentils?

She watched the boy as he moved away and then disappeared from view.

Preparing the flour did not take her any time: she took herself off to the grain merchant, bought what she needed, went to the mill, then came back. She was short and squarely built and corpulent. Her large breasts hung down and touched her stomach. She hurried off in the direction of the bakery of Umm Sayyid. There she announced that she was going to bake her bread right away and anyone who wanted to fry any fish or bake any dishes of food would have to wait until after the bread had been done. She did not listen to any objection. Shaking off her headcloth, she threw it over her shoulder. Generally the bakery was empty at that hour of the morning—just one or two women sitting with Umm

Sayyid, who would gaze at Sakeena without saying anything. She returned home after saying what she had to say. On her way home she was elated with a sense of pride. She gathered up her gallabiya from one side, thus baring her plump leg, and fixed the pleat of the gallabiya with her elbow at her waist, so that as she walked the movement of her arms and feet was like that of a duck approaching the canal.

Half the bread baked was swallowed up through debts, and she added up what was left. "I get along all right, praise God."

It was enough that she was going to settle her debts, which had been long outstanding. She could always borrow when things became difficult. She put aside the number of loaves owed to each of the women, beginning to pay them back immediately on her return from the bakery. She went by herself to pay back the exact amount she had taken. It would not be right to send the boy—what would the women say about her? She wrapped each woman's loaves in her headcloth and made her way to her. It was not that she was hiding them from people's eyes—there was nothing to fear from them. She was just protecting the bread from the dust and the flies. "Also, it's not good to attract the evil eye." And one of them might be annoyed at seeing her loaves of bread exposed as she carried them on her arm.

The loaves that were left she kept in the palm crate that she hung by a rope from the ceiling, fixing one end of the rope to a nail by the courtyard, keeping the bread away from the rats and from the eyes of her husband and the two boys: even if one of them had just eaten, if he saw the bread within reach he would still eat all he could—her husband would finish it all off at one sitting.

The days when he worked did not last all that long. She would see him coming along with his gallabiya thrown over his shoulder, and she would be dejected, thinking about the baking of bread, with the loaves in the basket almost finished. It would appear from his exhausted face that he wanted to sleep. She would join him in the living room: he liked her to massage his back before he drifted off to sleep.

"What do you find enjoyable about sitting at home?"

He did not reply.

She leaned over him and her breast touched his shoulder. Again she asked him.

"I don't like anyone insulting my mother," he muttered.

"And who's insulted her?"

"The customers on one occasion, and once the owner of the café."

"And why do they insult her?"

"Ask them. Insulting someone's mother is something they enjoy doing."

He slept for two days and nights. She hid him a couple of loaves in a piece of clothing beside the bedding. She heard him crunching the bread when he woke up to eat, after which he went back to sleep. Sometimes he asked her if there was something to dip the bread in.

"Where from?" she says.

"Then an onion?"

"Where from?"

"Not even a bit of salt?"

She gave him the salt and he gulped down some water and went to sleep.

Her feeling of fury went away. Every time, he had some

16

sort of reason to give. So what if they insulted your mother or your father? Was that the end of the world?

"You listen to the insult and you just shut up."

A week—that was all he worked. It was enough for her to go once to the bakery. There were only three loaves left in the palm basket for the two boys, and then she would go back to borrowing and calling in at people's houses. If only he had helped her out with another week, or even four days, she would have been able to do another baking. "There it is, though—that's how things are."

He returned at night from his loafing about and sat himself down on the stone bench on the other side and stared into the darkness of the lane. "My goodness, if only I had a cigarette."

He looked at Ragab, who was lying beside her leg, struggling against sleep. She understood what he had in mind: he wanted to send him to the grocer's to bring him a cigarette on credit. "To you of all people he'll not sell on credit."

"I know."

The night was quiet, the moon was out and there was not a sound. Everyone was asleep. Who but them in the lane was still up at this hour? Colic brought on by hunger keeps sleep away. It would only be an hour or so and their stomachs would quieten down. Stomach cramps do not last—a twinge or two and they settle down.

Her husband stretched out his legs in a relaxed way. He was in a good mood—she did not know the reason, and she did not want to know. She had enough on her plate. There was not one of her neighbors from whom she had not borrowed some bread and not yet given back what she had taken. What about going to them once again? Maybe there were two of them who would not turn her down. They all knew that she paid back what she borrowed—it was the first thing she did on the day she baked bread.

"This time he's stayed home a long time," she thought. "There's not a thing on his mind."

His voice came to her faintly. "That's it, Sakeena." He gave a sigh and was silent.

She turned to him in surprise.

"Education's a good thing," he said.

Her surprise increased. "What education?"

"Education, woman—schools."

"Schools? Fine."

"Schools and universities. Tonight the students from the village who are at university came back on vacation. They were spending the evening at the café on the other bank, the big café, the one with a wooden wall round it."

"I know it, I've seen it."

"I was sitting on its stone bench next to the wall and listening to them talk. Oh, what talk it was—I'd understand some of it and there'd be things I didn't understand. I felt I'd like to ask them."

"And what is it you didn't understand?"

"As though you'd understand, Sakeena—just shut up."

"I've shut up."

"They say you shouldn't work every day like the buffalo at the water-wheel. You should have time for thinking. That's all very fine, but thinking about what? They didn't say. I just looked at them and kept quiet."

"And of course you enjoyed all this and understood it."

"They said a lot of things, like what are we living for? And I say to myself, what's it all about? You're just living.

They say you get married and have children. So what? And I asked myself, what more do they expect of us? A lot of talk. And after they went, I went too, with my brain boiling and spattering. What I say is that there are people who are contented and people who aren't. It's a funny world."

"And what's funny about it?"

"It just is."

He fell silent. Drawing up his legs, he went to sleep on his side, after which he stretched out on his back and began scratching between his thighs.

"The whole day I've been scratching."

He asked her if she had cleaned out his underpants before washing them.

"I cleaned them, Zaghloul—piles of fleas and lice. Be careful where you sit and where you throw them."

"I don't sit with anyone but you—and no one but you takes them off me."

"Who's listening? Since when? A month ago?"

"Woman! What about last Thursday?"

"And you count that? Anyone else would be embarrassed to mention it."

"It was just the once."

"Once? All night going here and there till your strength runs out—what am I supposed to say?"

He gave her a kick, which landed on her thigh. It was the first time he had kicked her. She curled up and kept quiet, while he stood up and walked off.

It was a bad day for him when he got to know the students. He went out each day at sunset and returned at first light. He looked for them throughout the village until he found them, and then sat not far away so that he could hear their voices. He did not want to attract their notice so that his presence would annoy them. Sometimes he realized that he was laughing when they were or that he was nodding his head in agreement when he heard something he understood and liked.

Occasionally he would not find them, and he would continue searching around for them until he lost hope and made do with any group of people he happened to come across, when he would settle down quietly beside them and listen. But he would not be happy with what they were saying, the same old talk they had talked before: So-and-so went away, So-and-so returned, So-and-so beat his wife, or she got angry and went off to her family's house, So-and-so had his animal stolen, the price of things goes up day by day, and what the ration grocer steals every month. He was not excited by anything he heard, and more than once he fell asleep and woke up when one of them shook him to stop his snoring. How could they compare with his friends the students? True, he did not understand all that much of what they were saying, but what he did understand exercised his mind for a long time, and even what he did not understand he found himself attracted to, enjoying his perplexity as he turned it about in his mind. Yes, and also their enthusiasm when they were talking, their voices mingling and becoming louder. He would nod his head as he listened to them with real pleasure. He liked the words "my friends," and he would go on repeating them to himself.

There were five of them, sometimes one more or less. They always gathered in the large café, in the same corner that overlooked the street. When he did not find them there, he would look around everywhere, sometimes catching sight of them walking along the road through the fields. The sounds of their loud laughter would reach him, while he was far off and could not hear what they were saying, and this would upset him, though he was happy just to be near them.

Sometimes when he did not find them anywhere, he would pass by their houses, having found out where they lived, and he would find them all gathered together in one house. He could distinguish their voices from hundreds of others. He would listen a little and would know from what they were saying that they would not be going out that night, and so he would go off and look for some other people.

Once he was sitting on the stone bench of the large café alongside the fence, while they were inside. They were silent, smoking water-pipes and coughing loudly.

He said to himself, "They're too young to be smoking. If only they'd wait five years, it would be better for their chests."

They were talking in low voices and he could not make out what they were saying. Then little by little their voices grew louder: they were talking about girls and women they had known at their universities in Cairo, Alexandria, and Helwan. One of them was renting a room in a flat without a door, a flat consisting of two rooms on the ground floor. The other room was occupied by a woman approximately in her forties. She lived alone and went out early at night, not returning until the following afternoon. On some days she stayed in her room without a sound being heard from her. She dressed modestly and did not wear any make up; she always had a green and black shawl around her shoulders.

They would greet each other fleetingly, but without saying anything. They both closed the door of their room. He was shy of her, not knowing anything about her. They had a shared toilet, and without any agreement on their part, each would give a loud cough so as to tell the other that they were on their way to the toilet, and after finishing they would close the door of their room with a loud bang to indicate their return. He said, "It's a lousy life."

And they asked him if he had slept with her.

"Sleep with her? She's as old as my mother."

"Older women are nice."

"Nice, and kind too."

"Listen to the rest of it." And he went back to his story.

For some reason, he went out one night directly after she had gone out. He saw her some steps ahead of him. He slowed down so that she might be far enough ahead of him. They reached the main street, which she crossed to the other side. He spotted her entering a café on the square there. Driven by curiosity, he followed her and entered the café. He was surprised to find her sitting at a table opposite the door. Their eyes met. Meeting her stern gaze, he was at a loss and seated himself on the nearest chair he found. After this she ignored him, not looking in his direction at all. He stole glances at her, and found her sitting with a man in his fifties or slightly older. His hand fell several times on hers as it lay on the table. He gently moved her fingers between his and then moved her hand away. When the waiter came with their order he leaned across slightly so as to put the tray down on the table and rested his free hand on her shoulder. After that she left with the man and the two of them took a taxi.

They shouted around him, "One of those."

"As soon as you said a green and black shawl I knew. There's not one that came to my place without that same shawl on her shoulders."

"And then?"

He went on with the story. He said that at noon the next day he was going out to the college and was closing the door of his room when he saw her coming from the entrance to the flat. She stood in the passageway between the two rooms. She was beside herself with anger and said quietly, "Would you be so good as to tell me why you were following me yesterday?"

He was confused and said that he had not followed her and that he had entered the café by chance and did not know she was in there.

She was still angry as she looked him straight in the face and said peremptorily, "Yes, I'm like that. Anything else you'd like to know?"

He was at a loss and wet with sweat. Without another word he rushed outside.

When he stopped talking, they shouted at him, "And then?"

"Yes, and then?"

"Nothing." And he laughed.

He said that the two of them went back to as they had been, exchanging greetings without saying anything, both minding their own business.

"And she didn't come to your place?"

"She didn't, and she had no intention of coming."

"And you didn't try?"

"Try what, my friend?"

He said that the only thing he was afraid of was that someone from the village would come to visit him and see him in this situation and that there would be a scandal, and so he began to look around for somewhere else to live. The day he was moving his things he was surprised to find her opening the door of her room and coming toward him. She was wearing her dressing gown over her house gallabiya, and her face was calm and sad. In a hoarse voice she asked him if she had done something to annoy him.

"Not at all."

"Then why are you leaving?"

At this he was frank with her. He said that she no doubt knew about the customs of country folk. His father or one of his brothers would certainly come to visit him one day, or would have something he had to do in town, and would stay with him for a day or two until he had finished. It was not be possible that they would not come to know of her presence, and he would be put in an embarrassing position, whether through the way they would look at her or their attempts to talk to her and give her advice, all of which would put him in a difficult position.

"I understand," she muttered, without looking at him. Turning round, she went to her room and locked the door.

After that, each one of the students told his story with women, how they had got to know them and then had sex with them, with or without payment, and the number of times they would do it in one night, and the positions they did it in.

"The biggest lie you hear is that they are all the same in the dark."

"That's right—no two are the same in anything."

"The best moment for me is when I'm undressing her bit by bit."

"Like in the films."

"Films maybe, but it certainly has the right effect."

"I'll cut my arm off if you've even touched a woman before."

"Look, after much experience I'd say there's nothing better than masturbation—alone with yourself, embracing together in a moment of white heat."

"You're dead right. I know a woman who told me that her husband leaves her in the bed and goes into the bathroom to masturbate."

"Ridiculous talk—from a degenerate woman. There's not a man in the world who would do such a thing."

Each of them would have something to say, and their voices would grow louder—young men. He used to be like them. He had got into smoking early on, at the age of ten, then he gave it up. And he had got to know women earlier than they had, when he was fifteen. Before that he used to spy on them at dawn on the river bank, when one of them would squat down among the trees along the river and strip down bare except for her slip, and throw herself into the water. The slip would become inflated while she was swimming and would be shifted onto her shoulder, and he would see her body all naked, wriggling under the surface of the water. Then she would come out and sit down completely bare, her slip sticking to her, hiding nothing, and rub herself with a clump of straw. Like them he would be breathing heavily. How easy it was here in the village to get hold of them. And they did not take money like the city women the boys had known. He could tell them many a story about things he had seen and heard: the fields of maize at night, the pieces of waste ground on the outskirts of the village, the abandoned waterwheel, and among the trees behind the grist mill. When it came to the mill, one of them would leave her grist with someone to keep her place and go off to the clump of trees, and there would be someone waiting for her there. She would take her time, and come back, gathering her headcloth round her head. It went on in all those places that no one went near at night, because of the talk about demons who would appear there with their annoying pranks.

Sitting beside the café with his head on his bent knees, overcome by sleep, he was neither content nor surprised. All they said was said by anyone. He wanted to hear something he did not know. Their evening was about to end; after a while the café would be closed, and they would all go off. They had said nothing that baffled him as on other occasions, when he would think about it all the time he was away from them. Last time, they were talking about something they called 'politics.' The whole of the evening they talked about nothing else: the state of the country and what it was going through and what it had gone through for hundreds of years. He felt as though they were talking about some other country he had nothing to do with. They were asking:

Why has our country, unlike other countries of the world, known long years of colonization—and the worst sorts of colonization: Turkish, French, English? And what will come after that? There is no doubt that the fault is in us, the people of the country—we are content with any situation, any rule. Where are the big revolutions we have read about in other countries that have forced out the imperialist and brought down corrupt systems of rule? Look at what we have: Some demonstrations in the streets, when the authorities will bare their teeth and send their armored forces out and the demonstration will be broken up. The Orabi Revolt of 1919, that is all we have had in our long history and civilization, as it is called, and then comes the 1952 revolution, the revolution of the military—and where was everyone at that time? At home in their houses, thanks be to God. They woke up the following morning to be told: corrupt government has ended, never to return and we have come to look after you, God be with you— and He is in the heavens a witness to everything. Just tell me a single country that has been ruled by the military for nearly sixty years. This is what I say: the fault is with us, the people of the country.

They get angry and he waits until their anger subsides. There is a long silence during which nothing is heard except for the sound of people sipping at their drinks. After that they start talking about the songs they prefer: Umm Kulthum, Abdel Wahhab, Fayrouz. He likes the singers they mention, though he has never stopped to listen to one of their songs right through.

The evening went by without any other subject being talked about.

Two nights later they came to the café. They drank and smoked water-pipes. They talked a little, and he understood from what they said that one of them was ill. He listened carefully, tilting his head in the direction of the café. They were waiting for him to return from the doctor, so that they could pay him a visit. They said that most likely it was something wrong in the liver: bilharzia. Which one of them was it? He did not know; he had heard their names before, and had learned them, but he did not know who was who.

When they left the café, he followed them. They walked along one street after another and entered their friend's house. It was lit by hurricane lamps. He waited outside. There were two trees on the side of the street, so he seated himself under one of them, leaning against the trunk, and amused himself by throwing the pebbles his hand could reach into the middle of the dark road.

He thought he would look at their faces when they went off, and he would know. Then he heard the sound of their laughter coming to him, and the loud guffawing of their friend.

He got up, dusted down his gallabiya, and walked off.

After that they traveled away.

He went back to loafing around in the souk street until he met up with Sheikh Radwan, a professor of jurisprudence and canonical law at the university. He came to the village in the holidays to see to his lands and other business affairs, which he did not divulge and which the villagers discovered by chance. Who would believe that he owned a cloth store called al-Nahda in the souk, managed by one of his mother's relatives from another village, or that he had a share in a business breeding calves? He bought them young and left them to the fishermen to raise, and then when they were grown he sold them and bought more young ones. The amount they had gone up in price he split with the fishermen, who had been responsible for feeding them. The villagers found out about this business when they spotted three of the fishermen sitting against the front wall of his house waiting for him to wake up. Someone, overcome by curiosity, had gone and sat down with them. Fishermen do not have the same skills in talking as the villagers. During their conversation they hid nothing from him—and anyway it was nothing that could harm anyone. They told him that they had come from their nearby hamlets to buy calves from the livestock market, but the money that the professor had given them would not cover the price of the number of calves they had chosen; they had made a down payment and decided to see the professor and take the rest of the money from him. They had also stamped their fingerprints on the ownership documents for the calves, and had thus saved him from making the journey to the hamlets.

The man asked them how much it cost to feed one calf for a day.

"Not much."

"How much?"

"Not much."

"About how much approximately?"

At this the three fishermen were seized by a sense of caution, and the one who was talking to him answered, "Nothing much."

"Nothing at all?"

"Just a little."

When they told the professor about the conversation, he had a good laugh. He said, "If he'd come and asked me, I'd have told him and if he'd wanted I'd have given him the names of the fishermen I deal with."

His house had two stories and was at the entrance to the village. Around it was a small garden with rose bushes and orange and lemon trees. Nobody went near them when they bore fruit, even in his absence. The fruit would fall under the trees and go bad, then become dry and light and be blown away by the winds. The car he hired on his arrival stood at the head of the paved alleyway that led up to the front door. He would come out first, followed by a tall woman and three girls, who were shorter than her. Then came the driver, who would be carrying the bags. The woman and the girls were veiled, with small holes in the face covering, through which the sparkle of their eyes could be seen. During the whole time they were in the village they would neither go out nor be visited by anyone. The windows were always closed during the day and opened wide at night after the lights had been turned off. Passersby noticed dark specters of heads and shoulders, and when the lights of an oncoming car lit them up they disappeared.

The house was always still, with not even the sound of a radio. So people nearby were alarmed when one night two successive screams rang out from inside, followed by sobbing, then silence. They stayed for a while, waiting for something to happen, not having the courage to approach the house and inquire. They said that it was the voice of the woman, a voice full of pain and with a heavy huskiness. The screams of young girls usually have a certain shrillness.

Those close to him, when mentioning his good qualities and by way of sympathizing with him, said that he was hoping to have a boy, but that God had not given him one, and he took it patiently.

When he sat with them he disclosed that he was continually thinking about who would inherit from him and take his name. They replied that there was plenty of time. He said in a tone of resignation that the womb that had been filled three successive times with females would never produce a boy, and his words became a maxim that was frequently quoted, though most people were unaware of its source; sometimes they attributed it to one of the imams.

Some of those to whom he had confided his difficulty felt that he expected them to say something, so they told him, "Sheikh Radwan, take another wife. Nobody would blame you for that—what you are asking is perfectly legal."

He stared into their faces for a moment, then lowered his head in silence. As they went away one of them whispered, "He's either done it in secret or he'll do it—I've known Sheikh Radwan for years."

A few months later, when what had been hidden had become known, the same man whispered, "Didn't I tell you so—he's married to three women."

"It's his legal right."

"God be praised! He hasn't had a boy yet—and the fourth wife is surely on the way."

They did not need to search around or ask questions. She came all by herself. They noticed that on every holiday when he came, the woman following him was of a different shape than on the two previous occasions; once she was accompanied by two young daughters and another time by a younger girl—and they were all fully veiled.

No sooner had he settled in than the sheikh of the mosque would hurry along to ask him to bless them with the Friday sermon and to lead the congregation in prayer.

"Of course, of course, this mosque has a special standing for me. The first time I attended prayers was in it. I was six years old."

The mosque was crowded to the full. Mats had been spread outside to cater for the worshipers who came from far away, leaving behind the nearer mosques. The prominent persons of the village had made donations for the purchase of new mats and for taps for people to make their ablutions, and for plumbers to clear the drains that were always overflowing and carrying their smells to the street.

Sheikh Radwan came in the company of two of his acquaintances, all burnished and shining, and swinging his arms as he walked. He wore a long outer garment with wide sleeves, and a caftan, and the shawl around his turban was sparkling white. No sooner had he climbed up into the pulpit than he became another man, not the one they had known all along. The smiling mien disappeared from his face, which took on a stern expression. The sermon he gave was violent; in it he attacked the enemies of Islam and those who, deliberately or not, were harming it, and he threatened them with the torture of the afterlife, and described—in great detail—Hell and its fires that never go out. He dealt too with those who were ignorant about their religion and contented themselves with doing merely what was prescribed, yawning as they performed their prayers, and in such a hurry that they were unaware of the true sublimity of the act.

The worshipers crowded around him following the prayers, asking questions, which he answered with smiles while at the same time making his way out of the mosque. Zaghloul was among them, attempting to get close to him to hear what he was saying, and discovering that he was merely answering questions which he himself could have answered just as well, about mistakes in making one's ablutions and in fasting. The sheikh mumbled his answers long-sufferingly. "The mistake is unintentional, and God is forgiving and merciful."

At one point a man came up and whispered some words in his ear. The sheikh stopped with head lowered and raised his voice slightly. "And you fornicated with her?"

"It happened, sir."

"Fast for three days. Perhaps God will forgive you."

"And after fasting can I fornicate with her again?"

The sheikh turned around in exasperation and saw a face suppressing its laughter.

"Basyouni?" he exploded. "You had me fooled, man." He took him in his arms, then released him. "I've so wanted to have a chat with you. Tonight after evening prayers, at the big mosque, we'll go over the past and have a good laugh."

Zaghloul stood in front of the mosque looking here and there. They were crowding around and asking questions, and they had no sensible questions to ask. The sheikh, instead of ignoring them, answered their questions. Zaghloul remembered his friends among the students—if only they were here, or just one of them, he would be able to ruffle the professor with questions of another sort. His knowledge was vast, and in his sermon he had quoted the sayings of many eminent scholars. But what had stirred Zaghloul's admiration was the way he had joked with Basyouni—and within the earshot of everyone. He had never expected him to be the friend of someone like that. Everyone knew Basyouni, and no one in the village took him seriously.

It was the same story with the students: on more than one occasion their talk left him in a confused state, with his mind all over the place. Then, in their last sessions they were talking about women and saying things that could be said by anyone, even getting excited about it, and shouting.

Bending over and picking up a stone, he threw it into the river, and discovered that he was following Sheikh Radwan, who was a few steps away, and in the company of two men. Then he walked by himself along the souk street and came to a stop in front of the cloth store, al-Nahda. He climbed the step and sat cross-legged on the bench in the passageway in front of the store. The bench was made for two, but when he had squatted down with his fat thighs there was no room beside him.

Zaghloul walked in front of the shop, then went back. He did so again. He saw the sheikh finishing a glass of tea and putting it under the bench. There were few customers around, most of them women, going up into the shop, some of them staying on inside. The thought went on pressing itself on him: why not talk with him? Just ask him something and hear what he has to say. He searched around in his mind for the questions that had baffled him, but found they had gone. Perhaps, though, when he started talking with him they would come back by themselves. A question or two might slip his mind, but there were many that stuck in his head.

A woman passed by him and went up the step to the shop. He was standing hesitantly a step away from her: she was corpulent, and her tall body moved swiftly and smoothly. The wrap had slipped down from her head to expose soft, jet black hair and the corner of a brightly colored head-cloth fringed with gold and silver spangles that glittered in the sunlight. Bending her left arm, she let it come to rest under her left breast, so that this became tautly full and rounded and could be seen to quiver. She entered the shop as though raiding it. Zaghloul glanced at her quickly, then returned his gaze to the sheikh, who had leaned forward slightly and was staring fixedly at the woman's back. Zaghloul squatted down not far from him, contracting his neck, which he had been moving from side to side. The sheikh spotted him and hurriedly muttered, "Who's that—the woman who went in?"

Zaghloul turned and saw no one. He went back to looking at the sheikh, who had settled again and whose eyes were now on the door of the store. Digging at the ground between his feet, Zaghloul said, "As soon as I saw you, sir, I told myself that you were the person to give me the right answer."

The sheikh glanced at him in annoyance and muttered, "Quiet! Later."

Zaghloul was deep in thought and did not hear him. "Many questions," he said. "They come and go in my brain. I told myself you'd explain them to me."

The Sheikh closed his eyes for a moment, then looked sharply at Zaghloul, who continued to burrow around between his feet.

"The Almighty," he said, "created the world and the people and everything, and He ordered them to worship Him. I ask myself, if He created all that, what did He want them to worship Him for? And if they don't worship Him, He gets angry and threatens them with torment."

The sheikh was wide awake on the bench; his eyes widened as he looked around him in surprise.

Gathering his gallabiya around his knee, Zaghloul said, "Just humor me, and explain it to me. If the Almighty wants them to worship Him, He should appear in whatever form He wants and say, I'm the one who created you, so worship Me. Then no one would say No."

He stopped talking and wiped his mouth with the back of his hand. He looked at the street and the people going and coming, then bowed his head and went back to scratching at the ground. On the bench, the sheikh's back was drawn tight and his face was coloring with anger. He stretched out his feet searching for his shoes, which were lying to one side under the bench.

"All right, so I'm not all that bright, but I do think. I say to myself, the Almighty sent a lot of prophets, one every few years, and I know three of these: Moses, Jesus, and Mohamed—may God bless them and grant them salvation. They all preach the worship of God—and each one preaches it in his own way. And those who follow one way say that they are the best in the eyes of our Lord, and they deny anyone else. Then with time we see the three lots all fighting and killing each another. And I ask myself, Why? If it was necessary, surely one prophet was enough."

As he talked he was oblivious of anyone around him. His first feeling was of surprise, rather than pain, when he found himself being given a kick that threw him several paces to the rear and landed him on his back. He bent his knees and raised them to protect himself. The sheikh's cry stopped all movement in the street and brought the

36

customers, including the women, out from the store. "Finding fault with our Lord, you son of a bitch!"

Zaghloul was able to avoid the kick that was aimed at his stomach. He stood up, held in the grasp of the sheikh, who was dragging him back to the bench. The sheikh was still in his stockinged feet, while his eyes searched around for his shoes, which he perhaps wanted to beat Zaghloul with, having beaten him with his hands.

"Where've they gone?"

Zaghloul spotted the shoes and pointed to them hesitantly. The sheikh looked where he was pointing and saw them.

"You infidel, you good-for-nothing!" he exploded as he struck at Zaghloul with his fist.

Some people came running from the street, calling out, "Leave him to us, sir."

Savage blows rained down on Zaghloul, who could scarcely be seen among them. One of the customers had taken off her slipper and was shouting, "Where is he? Was he trying to steal from you, reverend sheikh?"

A nail protruding from the sole of the slipper pierced Zaghloul's head.

"You infidel, the son of infidels!"

Zaghloul's voice was lost among all the shouting and screaming, "The gallabiya, you're tearing the gallabiya!"

The sheikh drew him toward him as he raised his right hand to deal him a blow. On the middle finger was a ring with a large stone; for a second it gleamed in the sunlight, and the handsome woman standing by the door of the shop muttered, "Twenty-four carat gold—I know the way it shines, even meters away."

The sheikh was surprised to find how easily the gallabiya was tearing apart in his hands. Zaghloul's naked body was extremely emaciated, the bones of his chest protruding, his underwear mud-colored. Pushing Zaghloul away, the sheikh, breathing heavily, seated himself on the bench.

"The infidel! And he says these things to me, of all people!"

The others stopped hitting him: his nose was bleeding, there was a welt the size of a date on his head, his lips were swollen, and there was a red bruise around one eye.

"The gallabiya's torn."

He gathered up the two sides of the long tear around his body.

"Measure off five meters and hurl them in his face," the sheikh called out to his relative who ran the shop.

Zaghloul turned around and walked off among the bystanders.

The sheikh's relative shouted to him to wait while he cut him the cloth.

Zaghloul continued walking until he had crossed the street and disappeared into the lane opposite.

Sakeena was sitting at her place on the stone bench awaiting the breaking of day; her younger son, Ragab, was fast asleep, his head resting on her leg. As she pulled at his gallabiya so that it covered his thighs, she noticed where the boil still was. She thought that it would have gone by now. She touched it with the tip of her finger. "Still hard."

The boy moaned in his sleep.

Her husband on the other side of the stone bench was cleaning his teeth with a fresh piece of straw. Her other son, Zahir, was some way from them, resting his back against the frame of the front door. He was perhaps the hungriest of them, and did not stop running about. The lane from top to bottom was empty of anyone, not a sound, everyone asleep, the night's humidity making everything damp.

Two dogs ran gently along side by side, stopping to sniff around the thresholds of the houses, then continued on their way. One of them—presumably the male—jumped onto the other's back, trying to envelop it between its legs. For an instant the female lowered its head and almost gave itself to the other dog, then suddenly it wrested itself away, and the two of them continued to run on, close together. Sakeena looked away from them, thinking that the way the one dog had jumped onto the other had not shown much enthusiasm. She folded the gallabiya around her legs. "It won't be long now—an hour more at the most."

They would wake up, wash their faces, have breakfast—with tea if there was any—like all of God's creatures, and the men would go out, at which time she would go to the women. When she had plenty she would not neglect a single one of them. They had come to her before and they knew. The last time was when Zaghloul had worked for two whole months, and there was everything in the house: a woman came and asked for sugar and tea, enough for the pot that was on the fire, and with the guest sitting there, and with no one available to go to the shop. The sugar and tea for the pot was never given back, nor the coffee for the coffee pot, nor the salt, nor a couple of cloves of garlic, nor the onion. Many things were given and not returned, even the oil. "No, not always with the oil."

If they came with a glass or a mug, then that would be a

loan, and if they came with a saucer—just enough for the cooking that was on the fire—it would not be returned. She gave them everything they asked for, whether it was a loan or not, and those who gave it back that was fine by her, and those who did not—that was fine too. And she would not say a word to her, or give her a look.

For two whole months there was everything in the house that one could wish for. When they had a half-kilo tub of sesame seed sweet, she locked the door on herself and the two boys—Zaghloul was out at work and they saw him only occasionally—and they finished off the tub in one sitting. During those days she bought two gallabiyas and two sets of spare underwear for Zaghloul and the two boys, and for herself too, and slippers for Zaghloul—only the second time he had worn slippers, if we are to reckon the first: it was the day of his marriage and he borrowed them from one of his friends. He had given them back the following morning, and his friend had said, "Hang on to them for a couple of days—you're still a bridegroom."

The second time, she bought them for him. She wanted to see him wearing them. After a couple of days he lost them, returning at night barefoot. It was she who noticed, and she asked him about it. He leaned over in surprise and mumbled, "Yes, that's true—where have they gone?" He had left them someplace—and the places he went to were many. He tried to remember, and he went back to look for them, but returned without them.

Ah, mercy on Hagg Abdul Raheem. She had not heard of a better man. She wished she could have seen him, but she did not. Zaghloul had worked with him by chance. He had been abroad for many years, and before returning he

40

had renovated his house, building a wall at the back that took in a part of the canal bank to annex it with the house. And not a soul said a word about it.

This is what she heard—though she did not hear it from Zaghloul. He would not say a word, even if she asked him about the Hagg or his house and what went on there.

Zaghloul was out looking for work after he had stayed at home a long time, apart from the evenings he would spend on the streets. Hagg Abdul Raheem had returned from abroad. Everyone who saw him was surprised at his size, which had increased fivefold. His neck had disappeared and he had a rattling in his throat—it was said it was caused by some illness—and his feet were no longer capable of carrying his weight. When he needed to leave the house, the neighbors brought a mule and stood it in front of the threshold of the house; he would come out supported on the shoulders of two men who would help him mount the mule, his legs hanging on one side.

Zaghloul happened to be crossing the souk street and saw the mule coming right by him. He stopped to let it go past. He did not know the Hagg, or even his name. He saw that he was sitting on the mule awkwardly and might fall off at any moment. He gently stopped the mule and turned to the Hagg, who was in a state of alarm, grasping onto the saddle with both hands. "Lean on my shoulder and put your left leg across," said Zaghloul.

The Hagg settled onto the back of the mule and gave a relaxed sigh. Zaghloul was just about to go on his way when the Hagg stopped him and asked him his name and what he did.

"What do I do? A bit here and there—anything."

The Hagg looked him up and down and said, "Would you like to work for me?"

"Doing what?"

"This."

"This what?"

"Helping me up on the mule, and helping me down."

He said he was looking for someone of his size who could take his weight. People who were too tall were tiring for him when he supported himself on them, and his neighbors were all useless, and he might not find anyone when he wanted someone. He also needed someone to be with him when he went out.

And so it came about.

Early in the morning Zaghloul took the mule to the canal, washed it over, and gave it fodder. He cleaned the saddle and prepared the mule for riding. Then he sat himself in the courtyard near the Hagg's room and waited.

The Hagg did not go out every day, but he needed Zaghloul when he wanted to get down off the bed to go to the bathroom. Zaghloul took him there and then called to the wife to go in to help the Hagg in rinsing himself clean with water.

Her room was at the other end of the courtyard. Zaghloul would clap several times before she answered him. An old woman, a relative of hers, lived with her. She had an insolent way of talking and would say when she saw him, "Man, you hardly stand out above the ground."

She told him that since returning to the village the Hagg and his wife had had separate rooms: the bed was not large enough for the two of them, and she could not sleep for his snoring. She told her if the bed was not big enough for the two of them when she slept beside him, she should sleep on top of him!

She laughed and struck Zaghloul on his chest with the palm of her hand.

It was she who brought him something to eat, and his tea, and she sat with him in the courtyard until he finished. If it had not been for that mouth of hers, which never stopped talking, he would not have minded. When she opened it she revealed teeth yellowed by snuff, and when he ate he would avoid looking at her.

After two days the Hagg suggested he spend the night there, because he needed someone at night to take him to the bathroom. And so it came about.

He prepared a mattress in the Hagg's room. The sound of his snoring was very loud, but it did not stop him sleeping. On the first night, the Hagg woke him up and leaned on his shoulder to walk along cautiously to the bathroom. Then Zaghloul went out into the yard and clapped his hands close to the door of the wife's room, and went on clapping, but no one answered. Then he heard the Hagg's voice coming to him from the bathroom. "She won't answer you."

Zaghloul continued clapping, then called to her. "Ya Hagga! Ya Hagga!"

The old woman answered from her room. "You tiny little man, why don't you go in with him? Men together, what's the problem?"

He did not see the Hagg's wife going to him in the bathroom: it was the old woman who answered his call. And after this night, she too gave up going.

When Zaghloul had been there a week, the Hagg said to him, "Happy, Zaghloul?"

"Thanks be to God."

"I too feel comfortable with you." After a short silence he went on, "It's been a week, and you haven't seen your children. Here's something." He gave him a handful of loose coins from his pocket without counting them.

"Buy them something, and come back at sunset prayers— I have to go somewhere." He pointed outside the room. "Take the leftovers from lunch—I've told her."

By this he meant the old woman, and Zaghloul found her standing in the yard holding the package of food. "Enjoy it, and when you get back tell me what you did with the children." She went off laughing.

It was a joy to enter the house. They all gathered round the parcel of food. When Sakeena saw the pieces of meat she called out to the two boys, "Close the door."

Rice, okra, and bits of baklava, which Sakeena put to one side for when they had finished the cooked food. She looked at Zaghloul, who said he had already eaten there.

"And do you eat this every day?" asked the younger one, his mouth full.

Zaghloul got up and went to the living room. Sakeena watched him, trying to make out from his manner whether he would be wanting her, but she did not discern anything that would give her an idea, so she gave her attention to the food.

He handed her the money when they were on the stone bench, the glass of tea beside him. He asked her where she had got the sugar and tea from, as he had not sent her any money.

"I had a little, enough for the glass of tea," she answered.

She added up the money and murmured happily, "It's a lot, Zaghloul—really a lot."

"He's a good man."

He remembered that his children had asked him more than once about what the pastry called hareesa tasted like. They had seen it at the confectioner's. He told his wife to give them money to buy hareesa. The boys jumped to their feet with shouts of joy. "And me too," she called out.

The boys dashed off. She thought he wanted to get rid of them. She looked at the glass of tea beside him and saw that it was still full, and whispered to him in a voice meant to be affectionate, "Why don't you drink up your tea?"

"Let me be—I'm thinking."

"Thinking again," she said in her normal voice. "The students have gone, and it's quite enough what happened with the sheikh."

"Shut up, woman."

"All right, I've shut up."

She pulled the gallabiya around her legs and turned away to look into the lane.

He had been thinking about yesterday night and what the Hagg had told him. He had been lying on his side on the bed, looking at him as he lay on the mattress. He had asked him about the boys and if they went to school.

"What school, ya Hagg? We're not people for schools."

The light from the lamp hanging on the wall was dull, merely spreading shadows that quivered here and there.

The Hagg, who had his eyes closed, said he had two boys, who lived and worked in Alexandria. They did not like the village or the people in it, and he had not seen them since he came back. Years ago, when he first went abroad, he

45

had left them with relatives in Alexandria so that they could continue their education there. He saw them in the holidays, and felt that they were becoming estranged; even their letters became infrequent as the weeks and months went by, until they stopped altogether. When he had become ill some years back, it became apparent that this did not upset them too much, and he told himself that all boys were like that when they grew up; they had other interests, and their relationship with their fathers became distant. "That's how the world is."

The boys came to pay him a visit abroad. They did not stay long. Every day they went off to buy things: clothes and gadgets for their relatives in Alexandria. Each of them had a list of the sizes and makes of things, and they asked him about the shops and places that would have what they wanted. He knew that there were two girls, relatives on his wife's side, who were earmarked for marrying his sons, but he had not seen them, and none of the relatives talked to him. He would not have objected if the two boys had informed him, so long as it was they who told him what they wanted. He still badly wanted their love, and wanted it to come by itself, without having to talk to them. But they went back and did not visit him again. They only got in touch with him if they wanted money, when he would send them the amount they asked for. Even after his return, and although they were both working, they said their salaries were insufficient. He heard too that they were preparing to marry, and nobody informed him what was going on. In his condition, he could not attend the marriage party. Why did they not hold it here? But of course he did not express his feelings, or let them know that he needed them. They looked after their own homes and what they had. Sometimes it occurred to him that they would sell everything when they inherited it from him. They once told him that times had changed and that land was not what it was, that business was the most important thing, and that a single decent deal could bring in more than fifty feddans could make. What sort of deals were these? He did not understand what they were talking about. He wondered what had made them like this. Was it education? But we were educated before them, and we did not become what they have become. Was our education different from theirs? Was it that times, as they said, had changed, and had everything changed with them? I don't know.

He fell silent. His eyes were closed and his breathing was regular, interspersed with a soft rattle in his throat.

Zaghloul had been curled up on his bed. He sat up, uneasy at hearing the man's secrets. Why is he telling them to him? He has friends. Why does he not tell them? Perhaps it is his illness. He found nothing to say to comfort him, and did not know whether to go back to sleep or to remain sitting there. The Hagg's voice came to him in the slight gloom. "And their mother."

Again he fell silent, and Zaghloul's anxiety increased: Is he going to talk about her too?

He was silent for a long time, and Zaghloul thought that either he was thinking the whole matter over and would not talk any more, or he had been overcome by sleep. But suddenly, he began to talk.

He said that he had married her long years ago and had been happy with her. One of her relatives had been seeking to marry her—oh, so long ago—but she had preferred him over this man. He had the land, the cheese factory, the apiary, and the job of an assistant agricultural officer, while her relative was an elementary school teacher who owned nothing but the house he lived in. He had something, though, that made up for all that—he was a dandy who combed his hair to the side and had a cheerful smiling face. The girls—those who went for their compulsory education—returned home having bought one of those magazines with pictures of film stars and singers, and sat on a chair in front of the house, rather than on the stone bench with their father or mother, neither of whom knew how to read or write. They would be proud of the girl and of the magazine she was holding in her hand. Her mother would have allocated two of her chickens to her, which she looked after and sold their eggs—and that would be her pocket money. He laughed with a rattle in the throat. And from her pocket money she bought velvet slippers in blue or red, and ribbons of the same color for her hair. He gave another laugh. Perhaps you've seen such girls in your wanderings in the lane, waiting on their chairs for some suitable fellow to come along and change their lives? They were madly in love with the teacher; when one of them saw him coming along, she would take up a pose in her chair, open the magazine, and become immersed in reading it, with a faint smile on her face, pretending not to have seen him. But she would not be patient all that long and would soon steal a look at him. She would intend it to be quick, so that he would not notice, but her eyes would fasten on the man's handsome face until he had moved on. His wife had told him such things years ago. She had admired him too; she did not tell him, but he sensed it.

One day she showed him a piece of paper—yes, she was tidying a drawer in her cupboard, beside a small bag that was open, in which she kept small things: pictures, silver bracelets, keys. At that time he was working abroad. He heard her laughter, and saw the piece of paper spread out in her hand, an old piece of paper of faded pink. It had been folded over some ten times.

"Would you like to see something?" she had said to him.

"What?"

"Something from long ago."

Five lines. He remembered some of the words: My inspiration . . . your phantom never leaves me. And it was signed by her relative, the schoolteacher.

"A letter?" he asked her.

"Not a letter!" She laughed and said, "This piece of paper he put into my hand as he was leaving our house one night."

"Before I knew you?"

"Two or three months before that. Look at the lovely things he said."

He asked her why she kept it, and she said that every woman always keeps such things. This was understandable, and he returned the piece of paper to her. She folded it back as it had been, and put it away in the pocket of the bag. She did not go on arranging her things, but gathered them all up together and threw them into the drawer and locked it.

What brought this to his mind now? Sometimes he recalled incidents that happened years ago and that he thought he had forgotten.

Since their return, he had seen his wife only the once, and this just fleetingly. She had spotted him, it seems, coming out of his room and supporting himself against the wall, while she was in the courtyard, and had hurried to her room. And why should she flee from him? He did not understand and did not ask. She went to visit her relatives without informing him—it was up to her. She was accompanied by the old woman, and the two of them spent their evenings together there. She had never been fond of them. And the old woman? I don't know where she came across her, among all her jumble of relatives, to bring her along. They are inseparable: they eat together and go out together, and sleep in the one room together. How does she put up with her? I don't know. And the old woman tries to remind me of days I don't remember. She says I used to play in her house with the school-teacher, who was her relative. We were young, and we made a train, and we went from room to room imitating the train's whistle. And she tells me stories about naughty things I did and I don't remember them. I'm confused at the expressions of satisfaction on her face as I fall about between the walls of the bathroom, although at the last moment she always catches me. I tell myself that perhaps I imagine things, that there is no reason for her to be annoyed with me. And I can't remember having seen her before.

When he wanted to go to the bathroom his wife sent her to rinse him clean with water, and she was happy for him to be naked in front of her, and to stretch her hand between his thighs and buttocks. Somebody in his state accepts what comes. For him it was all one and the same:

if it was the old woman or someone else who rinsed him clean, what did it matter? Nothing upset him but for the smell of her mouth, and he was afraid that she might sense that. Even where his food was concerned, no one asked him what he wanted, and he ate what came on the tray. If they were things he did not care for, he left them, or if he was hungry he ate them just to satisfy his hunger.

He was silent, and remained silent for some time. But when the sound of his snoring rose up, Zaghloul stretched himself out with his face to the wall.

One day after the call to the sunset prayer, he told Zaghloul that he was going to sit for a while with his friends in the café. He was seated on the edge of the bed with his legs dangling down. He pointed to the wardrobe for Zaghloul to bring him something to wear. He brought him a gallabiya and a change of underwear. He helped him to take off the gallabiya he was wearing and handed him the change of underclothes, then he turned his back and waited. The Hagg said he could not bend forward to take off his drawers, so Zaghloul turned and pulled them off over his feet, leaning forward to allow the Hagg to seize hold of his back and shift feet.

They left the room, the Hagg leaning with one hand on Zaghloul's shoulder and the other against the wall.

The mule was outside, in front of the door. The threshold was slightly raised, which helped him to mount: the Hagg put his back to the mule and leaned on Zaghloul's shoulder, who leaned forward slightly and held the mule's neck to stop it from moving. Zaghloul raised himself slowly and the Hagg raised himself at the same time with his back until he was settled in the saddle.

The café he was heading for was on the river bank, with chairs scattered along its length. When the café owner saw the Hagg approaching, he brought a bench and placed it between the chairs occupied by his friends. Zaghloul took the mule there and helped the Hagg off it and sat him down, then he led the mule out between the chairs and left it to graze the grass on the bank, seating himself on a stone.

The evening gathering did not last long. On the way back, the Hagg remained silent until he was settled in his bed, when he gave a deep sigh and said, "Oh, I'm tired. It wasn't much of a gathering."

He said it was the first time he had taken part in a gathering of friends since his return—as you saw, I wasn't up to it. I would have been better off not to agree to go, and to put it off when they sent word. They had not changed. He had been away for a long time and had returned. There was nothing new in what they said, even the slanderous gossip they used to exchange in the past they brought up again and roared with laughter, even though they had already laughed at it many times before. He himself had joined in then with their boisterous laughing.

He asked Zaghloul if he had heard their laughter. He said that he had.

"Laughter with no soul," said the Hagg.

"It's still laughter."

"I don't seem to have the patience I used to have." He was silent as he stared up at the ceiling and then sank into sleep.

After that the two of them went out every two or three days. The Hagg chose the early morning. They made a wide tour along the agricultural paths, stopping for a rest among the clusters of trees and the fields around them. The Hagg would be slumped on his mule, while Zaghloul squatted beside him watching the frogs leaping about on the banks of the water channels. They did not talk much, being engrossed in their thoughts and looking around them.

One day they came to a stop under a mulberry tree. The Hagg gave a joyful laugh. "Mulberries—the last time I ate them I was ten years old."

Zaghloul sprang to his feet and began climbing the tree. "Here, take a handkerchief."

Zaghloul took the handkerchief and went on up. He moved nimbly between the branches as the Hagg watched him with a smile. He came back with the handkerchief full, and he held it up open to the Hagg, who said, "I'll eat half and you have half."

"You eat them all—I've eaten plenty of them."

"All right—I'll leave you just a couple."

He laughed and swung his feet joyfully. After he had finished he said, "Throw away the handkerchief—it's full of mulberry stains. If the old woman sees it, we'll never hear the end of it."

He stretched out his hand, trying to touch a branch. Losing his balance, he caught hold of Zaghloul.

"It would be great if we could come here again. We could bring something to eat and a sheet we could spread out on the ground to sit on. As for getting back onto the mule, by God, all you have to do is put a couple of stones one on top of the other and I could stand on them and support myself against the tree, and with the help of that shoulder of yours, Zaghloul, I'd be up on the mule."

One day, he said, "I want to see people, Zaghloul." So they went out together.

Zaghloul led the mule by its neck toward the souk street, which was as crowded as usual.

"There are more shops," said the Hagg. "In my days, the only shop in the street was the tailor's. Where's it gone?"

"A couple of stone benches ahead."

"Oh yes, here it is, but it's a different tailor."

"It was Usta Suleiman, but he passed away. This is his son."

"He used to make me gallabiyas, and then shirts, and not a single one of them was properly done. I used to hear that his sight wasn't all that great. . . . Now there's a place selling fruit juices, and a confectioner's, and a white-bread bakery. The village has grown."

"Hagg Abdul Raheem," came a shout, and Zaghloul saw a man hurrying in their direction.

The Hagg was staring at the man as he approached. "No way—it can't be! Atwa! I recognized you, just like you recognized me."

Atwa hurled himself into the Hagg's embrace as he sat on the mule, then led the mule into the entrance of a side street.

"This is my shop, ya Hagg. Sit a while and let's have a chat."

It was a fruit shop with crates stacked up on both sides. A boy brought out a bench, and Atwa brushed it over.

"Atwa, I'm afraid of getting off in case I can't get on again. You don't have a high doorstep?"

"I'll lift you myself." And he helped him to get down and settled on the bench.

"By God, it's been a long time, ya Hagg. I've really been wanting to see you. I'll tell you what—some mango to start with. I don't sell it to customers—it's just for friends."

He hurried off inside and washed a mango that he took from a crate hidden in the corner, under a pile of empty ones.

"Off you go," he shouted to the boy, "and buy a napkin from next door."

"But I have a handkerchief," said the Hagg.

"A napkin, ya Hagg—and a new one."

He drew up a low chair and seated himself in front of the Hagg.

"I'll tell you the truth—every time I think of paying you a visit, I say to myself. 'But it's been years, ya Atwa. Will he remember you? You've both been off in different directions.' It would have been really hard, ya Hagg, after all those wonderful years we spent together if you didn't remember me."

He drove away some flies that were hovering around the Hagg. "Ah, what days they were, I'll never forget them. Sometimes I remember things we did together, and I laugh, and I'm surprised how we did such things. We were the naughtiest kids in the village. You used to be the one to plan it, and we'd carry it out together. Do you remember when we raided your late father's garden, and there were mango trees—you always liked mangos—and your father found out? The guard told him. And the sound beating you got—I could hear your screams, and I hid. Not at home, and not in anyone else's house—I slept and lived in the mosque. No one saw me for two days. And the guard who discovered us—till the day he died he never knew where the stone that cracked his head open came from. He saw us together and looked at us, and it was obvious he knew it was us who'd done it. And throwing the stone at him wasn't enough for you, you wanted to put a snake down the collar of his gallabiya when he was asleep in the garden. And how long it took me to persuade you not to! You were keen on hunting for snakes. You'd get hold of one just under the head and hide it behind your back. There'd be a few people standing around, and you'd go and stand with them, and then you'd stretch out your hand with the snake, and the people would scream and run off—even the men would run away."

Atwa went on and on with his stories, the Hagg guffawing with laughter. He clutched his chest and spluttered, "Stop, ya Atwa—my chest."

"Fine, ya Hagg, I'll stop—God keep you safe."

He did stop for a while, then said, "All right, just one more, and that will be it. Do you remember Nabawiya and her boyfriend? His name was—I've forgotten his name."

"Mansour," said the Hagg.

"Yes, Mansour. So, you remember all right. What a bastard he was! Her husband was cutting the clover in the field, and Mansour was waiting for her under the sycomore fig tree by the broken-down waterwheel. She was sitting on the edge of the field, looking at her husband and then at the tree. Then she got up and said something to her husband and walked off to the tree. And our friend Mansour was sitting fiddling with his thing to get it ready—while we were up the tree. We'd seen them once from a distance, and knew what it was all about. We stayed hidden in the branches of the tree. When she arrived, and without a word she took off her underwear and threw it aside. Then she stretched out on the pile of straw, took everything else off, and opened her legs. Our friend stripped off his gallabiya, pulled down his underwear, and knelt on top of her. You stretched out your head and wanted to throw a sycomore fig at her, while I grabbed your hand. I don't know if it was the sound of the branches moving or the sound of the leaves, but she opened her eyes and saw us above her, our eyes looking right into hers. It took her a long time before she got her breath back and called out. Our friend leapt up from on top of her and went off at a run, falling down and getting up again, his drawers around his legs and no chance to pull them up. They kept tripping him up as he ran. The woman clambered backward off the straw and ran after him. Ah, what a day it was! And we climbed down from the tree and went to her husband in the field of clover. 'Peace be upon you,' you said to him. The man raised his head and returned the greeting, while you threw her drawers in his face and ran off. And every time I think of you saying, 'Peace be upon you,' I kill myself laughing. What did she say to him? God alone knows. But anyway, nothing happened to her. As I heard, though, it stopped her having children. She already had two boys—that was plenty."

The Hagg was out of breath from laughing, and was drying the tears in his eyes and waving his hand at Atwa for him to stop.

Atwa stopped talking.

After the Hagg's chest had settled down, they went out. Atwa carried him with the help of Zaghloul, and they placed him on the back of the mule.

The Hagg lay down on the bed, gave a sigh, and said, "Ah, ya Zaghloul, give me some water."

He drank, then stretched himself out, looking up at a corner of the ceiling, as he usually did.

"Ah, ya Zaghloul, what a great couple of days. If one were to die just like that, one wouldn't be too upset."

And that is just what happened.

He died on the following day. He had sent Zaghloul on an errand to the cheese factory, and when he came back he found a crowd of neighbors in the courtyard of the house. He spotted Atwa squatting in a corner sobbing with his two hands around his head. He walked in the direction of the Hagg's room and felt a hand seize hold of his arm. It was the old woman.

"Where are you going?" she whispered.

"To see him."

"May you see good health. Come along."

She led him toward the door and gently patted him on the back. "Goodbye."

And he went out.

The Wife

Sakeena was at her place on the stone bench. She was tired from waiting for the first signs of daylight. The sun had come up and people were still asleep. There was not the sound of a footfall in the lane. She was unable to wait. Her stomachache had lessened. It was bad at the beginning, as happened in the month of fasting. She bore the first few days with difficulty: a stomachache and feelings of dizziness. After two or three days the pains would go. It was how one became accustomed to it. Most of the days of Ramadan she would fast without having had the meal before daybreak. What worried her was the older boy. With the young one she could tell from the first glance what he was suffering, or even without looking at him. Whenever hunger tweaked at him he would cling onto her, and she would move about with him almost stuck to her. When he saw her sitting down he would hover around her, then stretch out with his head on her leg. It was the older one that puzzled her. For months his face had been changeable—one day it was dull and tired, and another it regained its healthy look. He no longer went near her to cajole her when he felt especially hungry, as he used to do. And when he sat down he became lost in thought and she had to call to him two or three times until he paid her any attention. At times like this, spittle ran down from the side of his mouth. She thought perhaps he had worms in his stomach, and if she was right he would not be able to stand hunger. If the worms found nothing to eat they would tear at his intestines. Zaghloul was in another world; there was no point talking to him. He sat at his place at the other end of the stone bench. He had finished cleaning his teeth and was now sucking at the length of straw.

She heard the creaking of a door. She knew the sound and where it came from. It was from the big house. At this early hour, the two girls made their appearance, old enough to work in the house. She did not know them, since they lived at the other end of the village, but she saw them as they went in, and heard their laughter, after which the door closed.

The big house was not far from her house, some thirty paces away. Around it was a broad empty space that halted the advance of the small houses of the villagers in its direction, as though there were an unseen line that must not be crossed, whether by their agreement or in spite of them, no one knew. It was said that Hagg Hashem, the owner of the big house, owned the empty area, having bought it the day he bought the land on which the house is built, as one lot, and he had the house built in the middle. From time to time someone came to sweep the empty space and sprinkle it with water.

The owners of the small houses were proud to be near it. They packed themselves closely together in the first rows, without leaving sufficient space between the houses, just narrow passageways that were barely wide enough for a donkey to pass through, provided the rider raised his legs onto its back. They enjoyed the empty space and the fresh breeze that came from it even in the heat of summer. Also, their forward position allowed them a view of the visitors to the big house from the cities; the women wore short dresses and high-heeled shoes and their heads were uncovered; sometimes when a strong breeze blew, their hair would be blown about and their dresses filled with air, revealing their naked thighs, as they screamed and attempted to wrap themselves up.

Sakeena's house was in the middle, but she chose her place to sit on the stone bench so that she could see along a straight line through a gap in the first row of houses to the front of the large house, with its door, and those coming in and out.

The house was pink, Sakeena's favorite color. She wished she had a pair of pink drawers, and she had in mind—if she ever had a couple of piasters to spare—to buy herself some cloth and run up a pair.

Sakeena had seen the house when it was a single-story building, with two lines of high eucalyptus trees on each side, which then grew densely in the empty space behind it. Now it was two stories. The second floor had not taken long to put up, and looked imposing after it was completed. Its pink color that she liked so much was radiant in the empty space, and there was nothing to conceal it from her eyes. Around sunset she enjoyed looking at it as the shadows of the eucalyptus trees moved over it.

When the building was finished, she waited to see faces on the large balcony or in the broad windows, but she saw none. Days went by, and months, and still no one: the upper floor remained empty. It seemed that the people of the big house had gone on living on the ground floor. Even the two girls and the boy, for whom the second story had been built—for when they came home for the holidays— preferred the rooms they had known since they were young.

What she knew about the house she had come to know by hearsay: a large, leveled courtyard, with five rooms on its two sides: the storeroom, the boy's room (though he was no longer a boy, but was working as an engineer and was married and living in a city two hundred kilometers away), then a room for each of the girls (both also married, one a doctor and the other a secondary schoolteacher, and living in different cities), and the fifth room, belonging to the elderly lady. By way of a small passage, the courtyard opened onto a spacious hall for visitors, its floor of colored tiles; at its curved end the Hagg's room.

The women who had entered the house talked about what they had seen in the way of furnishings, chairs, ward- robes, and brass bedsteads, but they did not talk about its people. These women included the egg-seller, the woman who traded in cloth and who came with special orders for the elderly lady, and Umm Khalid, who provided her depilatory services to the women of the notables and the civil servants and would make her appearance in front of the big house when the two daughters of the Hagg and the son's wife came on holiday.

Sakeena wanted to go into the house and see for herself what she had heard about it. She thought of a thousand pretexts, and every time she came or went in the open space, passing in front of the closed door, she tried with the two girls who worked there. More than once she stood in their path as they were going home and tried to start a conversation with them, but the girls only slowed down a little, gave her a look, and continued on their way without answering her. After that, whenever they spotted her coming toward them, they entered the first lane they came across, roaring with laughter.

Every two or three days one of them went out in the late morning, carrying a large bundle. Sakeena knew the bundle, and had seen it more than once: an old piece of rag, full of odds and ends. She was astonished at the amount of stuff that was thrown away. The girl went with the bundle to the refuse dump beyond the open space and emptied it, then returned with the old rag in her hand. Sakeena called out to her younger son, and no sooner had the girl entered the house and closed the door than she sent him off to the dump. "Have a look, see what they've thrown away today."

The boy went off and came back with old bottles and empty jars; and when she had collected a quantity of them she sent them off to the souk, where there was always someone to buy them.

One day the boy came back from searching through the rubbish with an empty kohl container. It was nicely shaped, and she had not seen one like it before. She could not decide whether to sell it or keep it, but she did not use kohl herself. It occurred to her to take it back to the big house: it had no doubt fallen among the things to be thrown away by mistake. The idea pressed on her, so she wrapped a scarf around her head and went off there. One of the two girls opened the door, while the other came up slowly. Sakeena stretched her neck and looked in amazement at the interior: all sorts of things here and there that she could not take in at a fleeting glance. She realized that the girl was asking her what she wanted.

Sakeena replied that she wanted to see the lady of the house.

"What do you want to see her about?"

"I want to see her about something."

The girl tilted her head to one side and there was an uneasy look in her eyes. "What exactly?" said the girl.

Sakeena did not want to antagonize the girls, so she opened her hand and revealed the kohl container. "It was among the rubbish," she said.

"Oh yes, it was me who threw it away—it's got a hole in it."

"You threw it away? I thought it had been thrown away by mistake."

She returned her gaze to the inside of the courtyard. The girl did not allow her to take her time, and said rudely, "So it's you who searches around in the rubbish each time."

"Not at all—I don't even see it. It's just this once that I was there and saw the kohl container."

The door was closed behind her. However, the girl had revealed herself: she must be getting someone from her house to rummage through the odds and ends, but when he goes there he finds nothing worthwhile because Sakeena's son has always been there before him. The two girls always leave the big house empty-handed, not wishing to carry anything with them, even if it is broken or of no value, in case someone in the house thinks that they are hiding something valuable. Sakeena went on thinking about this, telling herself how easy it would be for the two girls to shove something they wanted among all the rubbish. She would tell her son to look through the rubbish two or three times. And perhaps she would go there herself. She was convinced there was nothing wrong with the kohl container, but back in the house she filled it with water and watched disbelievingly as the water trickled out of a hole in it.

"So, even if it has a hole in it, we'll block up the hole with something." And she threw it into a corner of the courtyard among a heap of other things.

One day she was passing and noticed that the door was open. She hurried and went in but after she had crossed the threshold, she was surprised by the elder daughter, the schoolmistress. She knew it was her from what she had heard about her: tall, very thin, just skin and bones, with no breasts, just two little lemons, and an emaciated face. She was wearing a dress over the house gallabiya. Sakeena was confused at seeing her, and said, "The door was open . . . I thought . . . Is there anything I can do for you, ma'am?"

The daughter looked at the two girls questioningly, and one of them said, "She lives over there." And she pointed toward the houses.

"Thank you," said the daughter.

Sakeena remained standing there as though she found it difficult to leave after having gone in. She adjusted the scarf around her head. She looked at them and they exchanged glances. Slowly she turned around. She expected to hear someone call out to her as she left, but all she heard was the sound of the door being closed.

"It's always like that, they close it," she said to herself.

She did not cease her attempts. She hovered around. When there was enough bread in the reed basket after baking, and everyone had had enough to eat, she took herself off there, walking a little among the eucalyptus trees, moving the dry leaves aside with her foot. "No one sweeps here."

She glanced at the second floor, with its closed green windows. "You could see the whole village from up there, quite apart from the fresh air that refreshes the spirit, and yet they leave it empty like that."

She gathered some small branches that had fallen and threw them to one side, then returned to her house.

One day she saw the door open. She hesitated. The older daughter had left for the city. She remained hesitant and took her time as she walked. The sound of loud voices came from inside the house, and the laughter of the two girls.

"What's going on?" she mumbled.

Passing by the door, she looked in. What she saw made her shove the scarf from her head and rush inside, exclaiming, "Leave it to me, the two of you, the leg of the sideboard'll break."

The two girls were pushing the heavy sideboard from its place, trying to move it into the corner of the courtyard. The old lady was standing enveloped in her dressing gown, her grey hair done up into a knot at the back with a black ribbon. Her thin face had a tint of yellow.

In her dash inside, Sakeena's shoulder had brushed an unlit lamp standing on a nearby table. The lamp lurched forward and was about to fall, when her hand caught hold of it. But its glass bulb fell down with a crash.

Sakeena bent over, saying, "Keep away, madam—keep well away."

With the palm of her hand she went on sweeping up the scattered glass into a pile. Some of the pieces cut her hand and drew blood. She looked at her hand fleetingly and went on gathering the bits of broken glass together, then shoveled them into her lap. Lifting up the end of her gallabiya, she said, "Just a minute while I throw it away."

She went outside and emptied what she was carrying by the wall. She was dusting off her gallabiya when she heard the sound of the door being shut. She turned around and looked uncomprehendingly at the door. "Don't they have anything to do but close the door?"

After that she took against the big house and no longer went there, nor watched its door. Her quarrel with the place went on for more than a month until the day the provisions were shipped out.

She was sweeping the courtyard and heard the noise of vehicles entering the empty space. "Zaghloul!" she called out. "The provisions, ya Zaghloul."

Zaghoul came along from where he was lying down in the living room. He leaned over the stone bench to get a straight line of sight between the houses, and saw the three pickup trucks standing one behind the other in front of the door of the big house.

"They're the same trucks," said Sakeena, sitting down in her usual place.

Zaghloul went back to the courtyard and took two whole loaves from the reed basket, then squatted in the place he had tested the view from, placing the two loaves in his lap. Sakeena saw the loaves, but did not make her usual fuss by telling him to take only one loaf and to remember the children.

He waited until her eyes were no longer on the loaves before stretching out his hand and breaking one of them gently so it would not make a noise. He was afraid to ask for something to dip it in while the effect of his taking the two loaves had not yet worn off.

"There's a piece of pickled cucumber—you'll find it on the window," she said without his asking.

He jumped up, lifting the lap of his gallabiya with the bread in it, and found a small square hole in the wall of the courtyard, closed by a wooden door. He opened it and took out the cucumber, which was wrapped in a piece of paper. He felt into the hole, telling himself that sometimes there was a drop of treacle there, which she would be hiding for the boys. His hand came in contact with another piece of paper with crumbs of cheese that had hardened, and he took this too. There was a third piece of paper containing a little sugar mixed with tea, and this he returned to the hole, leaving it so that she could make him a cup of tea when she had recovered from her bad mood.

He went back to where he had been sitting beside her. It was the sixth time that they had witnessed the shipping of the provisions. Every four or five months the three laden trucks would travel to the son and the two daughters, each in a different city. He knew a lot about what the trucks carried because it once happened that he was passing by and had helped load them.

They saw the first truck, whose three sides had been lowered.

"Which of the children would you say that truck's for?" said Sakeena.

"Let's see what's put on it first. They're all the same anyway."

"No, it's different for the boy. Do you remember? The honey's more than for the two girls, and the pigeons too. See the crate of pigeons? It's the first thing they're putting in the truck."

"Then this is the son's truck—he wants to strengthen him up."

"But what about you, Zaghloul? You've never eaten pigeons and you're as right as rain." She leaned over and hit him lightly on the shoulder.

"And a crate of ducks, and chickens. Fancy that! A crate of quails this time."

"How do you know they're quails?"

"I saw them once—they're smaller than pigeons."

"Have you eaten them?"

"Never. Those who have say the flesh is soft and tasty. And they do wonders for a man."

She leaned across to him slightly. "What do they do?"

"Why should I tell you? You're getting quite enough."

"Go on, tell me."

"They say that a man doesn't get up off her the whole night."

"So? What about you, man, without any quail . . . ." She joshed him gently on the shoulder.

"And a can of cheese. And honey. And treacle. Everyone's carrying a can on his shoulder. The day I helped them they made me carry two cans at a time. A jar of cooking oil. And butter."

"And they eat all these things? It's how many months—four?"

"Them and their close friends there. And what's in that can? Maybe its ripe cheese. A crate of mangos. And guavas. And what's that a crate of, Sakeena? Something I don't recognize."

"Nor me."

"And a crate with straw in it—that's the eggs."

"And there's the sack of rice. The last time they brought that first. Then there's the sack of lentils. And the mashed beans. The sack's got a hole in it, and the beans are spilling out. I knew it was beans."

"A lot's fallen out. Of course they'll come back. And the bag, they'll stitch it up. One of them's picking up what fell out, and they'll put it back in the bag."

"And what will they do there with the mashed beans?"

"They'll make busara—I hear the town folk like it a lot."

"And do they know how to make it?"

"They have a girl they took from the village."

"By God, they've given me an idea—I'd like to make it. The last time I made it was a year ago, and you ate two platefuls on your own."

"Have you seen the two trucks for the girls? No crate of pigeons, no quails."

"So the Hagg isn't happy with the two husbands."

"Or maybe he's not happy with the two girls."

"Ah, Sakeena, what a thing to come out with!"

"I was a blind kitten before I met you."

She let her head fall on his shoulder. He stretched his hand out inside her gallabiya.

"Your hand's hot," she whispered.

She slipped her hand under his gallabiya and rubbed her face on his arm.

"Quail, eh? They should see what I've got."

Leaning against each other, they entered the house.

The old lady died one morning. There was loud screaming, and in a matter of moments many people had crowded into the house and round it. The front door was wide open, and there were men and women dressed in black, and cars unloading friends and relatives and then going off.

Sakeena stood on the stone bench with Zaghloul.

"When I first saw her the sign of death was on her."

Zaghloul searched around for his gallabiya and shook it out. "Sew up the tear along the side," he said.

"Are you going over there?"

"Here it is."

"I'll bring a piece of thread."

She went to the neighboring house and came back after a while with the thread wound around her finger.

He went off to the big house.

She stood and watched what was going on. On the second floor, the windows had been opened and a woman was cleaning off the dust. There was no sign of the two girls; no doubt they were busy on the ground floor. That's right, who will look after the house now that she's gone? The carts came in carrying the cloth for the awnings and the wooden beams and the chairs. She looked around for her husband. Not seeing him, she sat down.

Zaghloul returned late at night. Sakeena was sitting in her place on the stone bench, her head resting against the wall. She was fast asleep but woke up as he approached. "It's over?"

"What's over?"

"The condolences?"

"Long ago."

"You went into the house?"

"Went in and came out—several times."

"All of them are there?"

"What do you mean by all of them?"

"Her children."

"The two girls are there, the boy's coming tomorrow."

"And the place was full?"

"Packed. We set out thirty chairs in the open space and there were still quite a few standing. I was standing by the door, and I saw someone signaling to me. I went over to her—it must have been the older daughter."

"Unpleasant, was she?"

"Yes. She had me carry the dining-room chairs, and I went out with them to the people who were standing. Six chairs, but there were still a couple of people standing. I went in after her and dragged along two of what they call armchairs. All the time she was sitting on a cushion by the door. She said, 'Stay close by me.' And so I was coming and going. 'At your service.' Jugs of water. Glasses. Ashtrays, and four small tables that they asked for. 'And look after these things here, take them back yourself.' 'At your service.' 'And what's your name?' 'Zaghloul. Here, Zaghloul,' and she stretched out her hand with a packet of cigarettes. When I refused, she said, 'Go on, take them, they're from me.' Yes, by God, that's what she said. And after that she asked me if I'd known the deceased. She said the word 'deceased' and burst into tears, while I stood there saying nothing. I hadn't known the deceased and hadn't seen her. And when she asked me later, 'Didn't you know her?' I said, 'Is there anyone who didn't know her? A good-hearted lady, and she always spoke nicely and would always ask about how I was and how the children were.' She listened to what I was saying and said, 'All her life she loved everyone.'

"She was silent and sat and looked out at the condolence tent. It had two openings, one onto the empty space for those paying their respects to enter and leave, and a slightly smaller opening by the door of the house for the café owner and his workers, with his set-up and things by the wall. And it was from this opening that she was watching most of the mourners and the Quran reciter too.

"She asked me if I'd heard him.

"'They say he's good.'

"'We brought him from the district capital—they speak well of him.'

"'It's the first time he's been to the village.'

"'The fact is, his fee is very high.'

"She was silent and I stood there quietly. She leaned her head against the lintel of the door. And then something quite extraordinary happened."

"What?"

"Well, . . ."

"Tell me, Zaghloul. I always tell you everything."

And Zaghloul said that she was sitting near the door silently. And after a while she asked him, "You see the gentleman directly in front of me?"

"I looked and saw a man wearing a suit. He had a chubby face, quite good-looking, with a very thin moustache like a piece of thread over his lip, and he was looking down at the ground.

"'Do you see him?' she asked.

"'Yes, over there, with a small table by his right hand.'

"Then she said, 'There's a tray on it with a cup of coffee. Isn't it a cup of coffee?'

"'Yes, it's a cup.'

"'Go over to him and make as if you're taking the tray away, and tell him in his ear, "The lady Widad wants you."'

"'And where's the lady Widad?'

"'That's me.'

"I looked at her and she looked at me and she said, 'Take care when you're whispering to him that you're not breathing right on him—he doesn't like people's breath on him.'

"So I did as she said, and the man turned his face away, and his complexion changed. He looked at me and didn't say anything—it was clear he was in a bad mood. All at once he got up. 'Come along.'

"I got up behind him and he took me to the back of the place. He stood and gave me another look, as though not knowing what to say. 'Listen.' And then he stopped. His hand was moving in his pocket, and his finger pecked at my chest. 'Tell her . . . .' And he paused again, then went on. 'Tell her it's over. The story's come to an end. Understood?'

"'Understood, sir—but even so, it's you who should tell her.'

"The palm of his hand landed on my cheek, and I stepped back a pace.

"'Do what I tell you to do—or don't do it. I've had enough of this place.'

"And he walked off into the empty space, while I just

74

stood there till he was far away, then I went back.

"From where she was sitting she looked at me, and it seemed as though she'd understood without me saying a word to her. She remained silent, and I stopped talking. After a while she asked, 'Has he gone?'

"'Yes, he's gone.'

"'He misunderstood.' She was looking at the mourners with her head against the frame of the door. 'I was only going to ask him about his children, and hear him give his condolences to me.'

"After a moment's silence she said, 'Years ago he was my fiancé—just my fiancé. We'd recited the Opening Chapter of the Quran together as an intention of getting marrying. That's what happened.'

"He obviously upset her, for her to talk to me and say the things she said. She looked at me, and her eyes weren't crying any more. 'All right, Zaghloul, thank you. Off you go, in case they want you for something.'

"And I left her sitting there and went off."

Sakeena took a deep breath and said, "What a story, Zaghloul! And at the mourning ceremony!"

"Death stirs up old wounds."

She saw him getting to his feet and asked him, "And the packet of cigarettes, did you open it?"

"It's still sealed."

"Sell it, Zaghloul. You smoke just to pass the time."

"I won't sell it. Every two or three days I can take a cigarette. And anyway, Sakeena, if someone gives you something do you go and sell it?"

"Well, so what?"

He entered the living room and stretched himself out on

75

the bedding. She stayed on the stone bench looking at the big house sparkling with lights, as sleep overcame her.

After a few days everything was back to what it was. Some men came and swept the empty space, and some women cleaned up the house. Sakeena could see their shadows at the windows of the second floor. Then the windows were closed. She saw the older daughter looking out from the front door; she sometimes stood with her dressing gown wound around her and a shawl on her shoulders, looking about her and at the tops of the eucalyptus trees, and then she would go inside and shut the door.

Two weeks later, she left. Sakeena saw her get into the car one day with her two sons, as the two girls finally appeared and stood by the door until the car moved off, when they went inside and the door was shut.

And who was looking after the house? Hagg Hashem looked as though he had some illness; she saw him approaching once when she was returning across the empty space. He was a large man, and he carried a stick that he leaned on in his slow, deliberate gait. She stole a glance at him—normally neither she nor anyone else saw him—and found that he was staring blankly at things, with an ashen face, and she told herself he must be in considerable pain. Praise the Lord—his wife had gone before him. When she heard the screams she thought it was him. And the two girls? Could they do it? The man needs someone to look after him with the house so large: a courtyard and a hallway and many rooms, she did not know how many. There was all the sweeping and dusting and washing and cooking and baking to be done—never mind the baking, the two girls could always buy bread ready from Abbas's oven, government bread as long as the Hagg liked it, or they could get someone to go to the bakery for them.

Sakeena was anxious, she could not stop her head from thinking. She sat for a long time on the stone bench, and she noticed that the girl no longer went outside with the parcel to empty it out on the rubbish dump. When they left the house at sunset, each one carried a small package under her arm, and they locked the door with the key. The Hagg, it seemed, made do by using the outer door on his side of the house, which opened onto the guests' hallway. He was there all on his own the whole night. If he was not well, who was there to help him?

One morning, Sakeena went to the big house. There were things she just could not keep quiet about, and it was up to her more than anyone else, because of what she had seen and understood, to let the two girls know what had to be done. It really was not right just to leave the house like it was.

She found the door slightly open, pushed it, and looked inside. She saw the two girls sitting on the bedding in the courtyard.

"Come in, Auntie Sakeena," said one of them.

So they knew her name.

All the things she was intending to say flew out of her head. It was doubtful whether she would be able to say anything of what she had in mind.

The two girls were sitting with their hands and feet stretched out; it looked as though they were having their breakfast.

"Have a seat, Auntie."

She sat down on the ground where they had pointed. In

front of them was fresh bread, cheese, treacle mixed with sesame paste, and fried eggs, six of them, with the yellows all intact and a slight steam wafting from them.

"Have you had breakfast, Auntie?" said one of the girls.

"Thanks be to God." She avoided their gaze.

"Have a taste."

She understood that they wanted her to share in the food. She was moving closer when she noticed the arm stretched out to her with a loaf of bread with a piece of cheese on top, of it, so she took it.

She ate in silence, somewhat taken aback, confused by their reception of her and the affection, though lukewarm, that she had been met with.

When the girls had finished the food, one of them said, "Light up for the tea, Auntie—the primus stove and the teapot are behind you. And after we have our tea we'll talk."

The two rested their backs on cushions behind them. "Take the tray and put it on the food-safe."

As she was making the tea, she learned from what they were saying that the girl with the big bosom was called Zubeida and that the other one was Zohra. She saw nothing in their words or manner that seemed wrong.

She came back with the tray and held out a glass of tea to Zubeida who said, "No, Auntie, each glass has its saucer that goes with it. The little saucers are in the drawer of the food-safe."

They had their tea.

Zubeida said that the Hagg had woken up—she had heard him moving about in his room. She would make him breakfast and take it to him. "Come with me, ya Zohra— and you too, Auntie."

She was silent for a moment as she looked around her and said that she had to begin doing the rooms.

"They're clean—just dust off the chair and the cupboards and anything you find. And tell us when you've finished. You'll find a towel in the entrance to the kitchen."

Sakeena entered the first room she came to, and stopped at the door in wonder: the bed with its brass posts and the surround decorated in shades of blue, and the mosquito net rolled up, and two armchairs—as Zaghloul called them—with a small table between them, a wardrobe with six doors, and a large sideboard with light dust on its surface. She heard the sound of the two girls coming from the direction of the kitchen. She wanted to be with them, to see what sort of breakfast they were preparing for the Hagg. They talked to her as though they were masters of the house. She knew they had been there since childhood, when they were about eight years old, now they were both at least seventeen. They had the right to order her about: Come here, go there, clean this. No, just being in the house a long time did not give them the right to order her about. They were no better than her. She should not keep quiet. All right, Sakeena, if you're not happy, get out.

She went on wiping away the dust. It collected in all sorts of tiny crannies. The eye could not see it, not unless you were actually looking for it. It was only with the edge of the towel that she was able to get it out.

Having finished the rooms quickly, she went off to her place in the courtyard. She heard Zohra tell her, "You clean well, Auntie—even the posts of the bed are sparkling." It was clear that she had passed through the rooms after she had done them to make sure.

"And now," said Zohra, "the courtyard. Sweep it and clean the bedding."

She indicated the bedding the two of them were sitting on, which was covered over with a sheet.

"Yes, and turn over the sheet."

"By the way," said Zubeida. "I told the Hagg you'll be with us in the house, you'll be helping us."

"And what did he say?" she asked eagerly.

"He didn't say anything. He knows. It's just in case he sees you."

"And where will he see me?"

The sweeping was finished, and the washing up of the dishes still had to be done. They were piled up under the basin. It looked as if they had been there for days; they were half in water so that the remains of the food would not dry up.

She rolled up her sleeves and tied the end of her gallabiya around her middle, then seated herself on a low chair, and dragged the dishes toward her.

"The Hagg is going out now," said Zubeida, "and he's coming back for lunch. Get a move on so we have time to do the cooking."

Can I get going faster than this? I'll see how it's all going to end. I saw them sitting on the bedding with their legs stretched out and their feet crossed and tapping to the songs they were listening to on the radio beside them.

When she finished the dishes, she turned her attention to washing the clothes. The basin was by the entrance to the bathroom. There was not much to be done. She lit the gas stove beside her and heated the water.

When she placed her hand in the washing she discovered that it consisted of the two girls' clothes: three gallabiyas each, and five changes of underclothes. Her hand came up with a pair of knickers, no more than a hand's span in width. It would cling to you. Where did they get them from? Perhaps now they were on sale in the village, or perhaps the Hagg's daughters had given them to them.

She hung out the washing on clothes-lines by the stairs, then seated herself in her place in the courtyard. The two girls were whispering together and laughing. "No, ya Zohra," said Zubeida, "you make the tea—Auntie had a tiring day."

"I'll make it—it's not tiring at all."

She made the tea and carried the glasses and the small saucers to them on the tray.

As they were drinking the tea, Zohra asked, "Do you know how to slaughter, Auntie?"

"Slaughter what?"

Zubeida laughed. "And what would you be slaughtering? Chickens, ducks, pigeons."

"I've never done it."

"Zohra, you didn't say what we should slaughter."

"What about the Hagg?"

"I asked him and he said anything would do."

"Slaughter two kinds."

"A duck and a couple of chickens."

"Yes, and we'll have okra with them—the Hagg loves it."

"All right, Auntie, take a duck and two chickens—the house is right ahead of you. Umm Khalil will slaughter them. She always does our slaughtering for us. And while we're at it, let's buy two kilos of sugar and half a kilo of fine tea, a kilo of okra, and half a kilo of tomatoes."

The poultry were in the palm-stalk crates in the store-room. She took out a duck and two chickens, Zubeida gave her a ten-pound note from a small pocket in the top of her gallabiya, and she went out.

She thought to pass by the house and take a look: perhaps she would find somebody there at this hour. Generally they did not go out—where would Zaghloul go? He was asleep. The boys had gone out, and he had gone to sleep. He was always saying he did not get enough sleep.

She was not away long. She put the things she had bought in front of the two girls, who were in their usual place, sitting and listening to songs. She took the birds that had been slaughtered to the kitchen where she put them in a basin, then boiled up some water and poured it over them. Then she sat down to pluck them.

She saw the two girls whispering away together and suppressing their laughter. Then they both bared their legs and ran their hands over them, and Sakeena understood what it was all about. "They saw me plucking the birds and it gave them the idea."

Zohra stood up and went to the kitchen. Standing behind Sakeena, she lit the primus stove. The smell of burning sugar spread, and she left the kitchen with a plate of sticky depilatory paste. She went to the nearest room, the older daughter's room, but Zubeida came along and motioned to the next room, the room of the other daughter, into which they both disappeared and closed the door.

So they were plucking the hair from their legs, she realized and was surprised. They had the time and they had the sugar, so what was to stop them? They did not go into the older daughter's room—they were frightened of her, even when she was not there.

The girls came out in a great hurry, each carrying a roll of clothing under her arm, and went to the bathroom. Their laughter could be heard coming from inside. Afterward, they sat on the bedding with the brush combing through their wet hair.

A little before mid-afternoon, Zubeida came from the kitchen where she had been preparing some food. She said that the Hagg had arrived. Zohra carried the tray of food into the room, and when she came back she said, "Let's eat too."

Sakeena was standing in the kitchen washing the dishes after the meal.

"Take the rest of the food with you for the children," Zubeida told her.

The joy that overwhelmed her! She had been thinking about what they would eat, having left them in the morning with empty bellies. The rest of the okra would do for the three of them, then there was the rice, and the bits of chicken and duck. If only she also had some bread. What was wrong in her asking for them? She found herself saying, "Miss Zubeida, do you think I could have a couple of loaves?"

"Yes, take them. And take a piece of cheese. But come over here, I want to tell you something."

She went to them with a small smile on her face and sat down.

Zubeida said that the Hagg had spoken to her just now when she went to fetch the tray, and said that he would like someone to sleep overnight in the house.

Sakeena did not understand. She was thinking about the food she was going to take with her, and the shouts of joy the boys would raise when she went to them.

"Yes, so what?"

"So, you agree?"

"Agree to what?"

"To spending the night here?"

"Why? What's going on?"

"Look, I'll explain it to you." She said that the Hagg did not want to spend the night alone. He had not told her why, but she knew. She had heard the reason from his late wife."

"His late wife told you so?" said Zohra.

"How could she tell me, ya Zohra?" And she began to tell the story.

She said that the older daughter wanted to take her mother to her house for a week or two as a change. The late wife said that she could not leave the Hagg on his own, and her daughter asked her, "Why not?"

"He's afraid something will happen to him, and there'll be no one with him. You know he's ill. His left arm doesn't move all that well, nor does his left leg. Something could happen to him."

"I didn't know about his leg."

"Yes, for a month. He says he wants someone to be beside to give him his last mouthful of water."

"What are you talking about?"

"He said it more than once. You don't go up to heaven until you've paid all your debts and had a final drink of water."

"That's the whole story," said Zubeida. "What do you

say, Auntie? Zohra and I can't do it—our folks wouldn't agree to it. And we're about to get married, and who would put up with a girl who spends the night outside her house? What do you say?"

"I have my children—and my husband. None of them will agree."

"Ask them. Maybe they could spent the night here with you and go off in the morning."

"And will the Hagg agree to that?"

"Why shouldn't he? He's lying in bed sleeping."

"But he should know."

"Of course he'll know."

"I'll see them and let you know."

"All right, the work's done for now."

Sakeena went out. She could not contain herself for joy: The cooking pot full of food was tied up in a piece of cloth. And Zaghloul and the two boys would sleep early in clean bedding and would have dinner and breakfast—and she would do something about lunch too.

Zaghloul stood there with the two boys at the opening of the front door to the big house waiting for one of the girls inside to take notice and see them. He did not dare knock at the door. They were all wearing gallabiyas and clean underclothes. Sakeena had prepared them for them in the morning. Before going out, she had told them they should wash their faces with soap, and she had left them a worn down piece of soap that she had wrapped in a screw of paper and stuck inside the window. She told them to be at the house after the sunset prayers.

And so it was. Zubeida turned around and saw them. "Go in," she said. And they went inside.

She examined them closely as they stood silently in front of her, Sakeena a little away off.

"Yes, Uncle Zaghloul," said Zubeida, her head raised and her arm bent at her side. "Come along, Auntie Sakeena."

Sakeena came and took them to the room of the Hagg's son. No sooner was the door shut on them than Zaghloul asked, "Why does she talk down her nose at us?"

"The fact is, she's wearing the late lady's dress, and she's not up to it."

The bedding was laid out ready on the floor: a wide mattress, pillows and a covering, and a warning from Zubeida to Sakeena not to use the bedstead.

The bedding was comfortable. Their bedding at home was straw covered with sacks. Sometimes there were bits of wood in with the straw, which they could feel pricking them before they went to sleep: they would put off looking for them to another day, and then forget about it.

The two boys rolled about on the mattress, and Sakeena asked them to wash their feet before going to sleep. She pointed at the old pair of slippers that had belonged to the Hagg's son. "One after the other."

"Are we going to sleep now?" asked the young one.

"Let's eat first."

"Is there any supper?"

"Yes, a supper you'll really enjoy."

She went out and came back with a tray full of food: what was left over from lunch, pieces of meat and chicken, and stuffed cabbage that she had taken the trouble to make during the day. After the food she took them to the bathroom, one after the other, each carrying the slippers.

They settled down side by side on the mattress.

She said, "I'll just see the two girls."

The young one asked her, "Are we going to be here all the time?"

"We'll see."

"And we'll have two houses, one for the morning and one for night."

She joined the two girls, and Zubeida asked Sakeena to leave the door of the room half-open, as the Hagg might need something: he would call her husband. She had told him his name, but he might forget it and call her name instead.

The girls wound their scarves around their heads. When they left the house, Sakeena closed the door.

Finally, alone in the house so that she could see it at her ease. She had already seen the storeroom and knew everything in it. The room of the late lady had been completely emptied. They had left the wardrobe and the sideboard empty and taken off the mosquito net and the surround from the bedstead. They had folded up the mattress with the pillow inside it and covered it over with an old sheet. There was nothing in the room for her to see, and anyway she was afraid to enter it at this time of the night.

The room of the older daughter; she would leave another room for tomorrow. She was disappointed to find that the doors of the wardrobe and the sideboard were locked. She looked under the bed: two large suitcases, also locked. She looked around here and there, wondering what she was looking for. She told herself it was just a peek; she hoped that she might see some of the daughter's clothes. The bedside table alone was open, and contained two pairs of shoes and a pair of felt slippers. She did not try any of them on, though she did find a packet of cigarettes in one of the shoes: perhaps she smoked in secret after locking herself in. The packet contained a lot of cigarettes. She took out a couple and brought a box of matches from the kitchen, as well as a small plate to act as an ashtray. Then she returned to their own room.

Zaghloul was elated to smoke one of the cigarettes. The two boys were fast asleep alongside him.

"Our house is better," said Zaghloul. "I feel at home there."

"I'm not used to being alone with you in a strange place."

"Yes."

"I don't even feel like doing anything with you."

"Same here."

"At least we have something good to eat."

"And I can't go in or out."

"It's been years, ya Zaghloul, since our stomachs had a decent meal, and if it happened it was just by chance."

"I'm locked up here till the morning."

"And what we have here is by chance too, but it might last a while."

"I can't even walk around at night, which I used to enjoy."

"The boys are eating, and they can't believe it. But their eyes are on the door—what are they frightened of? I don't know."

"I used to enjoy it—being with people and listening to them."

"So look around for work."

"As you say—tomorrow I'll go out looking for work till I find it."

"The boys will be at home for a while, and here for a while, and so things will go on."

"Yes, they'll go on."

Then they both went to sleep.

Waking up early, Sakeena swept the courtyard and arranged the bedding of the two girls and washed the dishes in the kitchen and cleaned it up, and the bathroom. Then she prepared the breakfast tray for them: fried eggs, cheese, and jam. She was swaying as she sang to herself while filling the plates.

She woke them up so they could wash their faces before eating, and they had a quick breakfast.

"Will we be eating like this every day?" asked the younger one.

No one answered him. Zaghloul smoked his second cigarette and asked if there were any more.

"When you come back I'll get you one."

He went out, and the two boys stayed with their mother in the courtyard until the two girls came, when they hurried outside.

The day went by, and other days, and Zaghloul worked at the café on the river. He had seen the customers there before and said that they were not the sort to curse people's mothers. No sooner was his first week over and a couple of hours before he was to receive his pay, one of the customers cursed his mother and father, but Zaghloul took it and shut up. He received his week's wages and remained in the job. He was content working in the café: perhaps it was mixing with people who came and went, faces changing, and being able to hear different things.

He chose shifts during the day so that he could be in

the big house after sunset. He would arrive just as the two girls were preparing to leave, and the boys would be there before him, all gathered together in the room around the food.

Sometimes the Hagg would go out after having his dinner, and Zubeida would tell Sakeena to stay awake until his return.

She went outside with her husband and the children and sat in the courtyard. Their voices were raised slightly, and she made them an infusion of fenugreek, which they had drunk before and were pestering her every day to give them. The boys rushed outside, and their shouts could be heard coming from among the trees, while Sakeena took Zaghloul to the second floor to have a look at the rooms there, all of which they found locked, so they sat themselves in the spacious living room, feeling the coolness of the floor tiles and looking through the closed glass window at the empty land.

"See, ya Zaghloul, the tiles are colored."

He cast a quick glance at the ground, then returned to looking outside.

"Every tile's got a rose in it," she said. "Do you see?"

She passed her finger across the lines of the rose, and Zaghloul turned to her.

If things had been in her hands she would have spent her whole life here. She found everything she wanted. But Zaghloul, after a day or two, stopped saying a word. He did not ask for anything, and took what came in silence. Even at home he did not say much, though his silence here worried her. He wore a frown on his face, and he could not bear any movement from the two boys, who were beside him in the bed. He would quickly scold them, and she was afraid he would go away and not come back. He would return to their house. But what did he have to eat there? The two boys would stay with her, only too happy with what they found here. And Zubeida, what was it she said? That Zaghloul's presence made everybody happy. Once she told her that when she went into the Hagg's room to bring him his tray of supper, he asked her whether Zaghloul was still there. And when she said that he was, she saw him give a sigh of relief. She did not understand what made him happy about her husband being there, but there it was. Zubeida also said that more than one woman who had her own husband wished she were in her place.

She was silent for a while, then she said something that surprised her—she wanted to tell it to Zaghloul, but she found him switched off, neither hearing anything nor interested. Zubeida said that the Hagg seemed not to be comfortable in the presence of any of his relatives. He had not hinted with a single word to her or in front of her that he wanted to invite them to visit. She did not know, and had not heard, if he had brothers or sisters. He may have had cousins on both sides of the family, but they were far away. She had not seen one of them in the house before. Perhaps there was a problem between them that she did not know about. He may have been frightened that that if one of them came to stay he would not leave after that if something should happen, God forbid. Things like that had happened and she had heard about them in other houses. He had not been open about it, but it occurred to her, she who had lived with them all these years, that their presence—and he knew better than anyone—would cause worry and unease. Anyway, that is what was said, after which she kept silent. The girl was bright and knew a thing or two, though it did not show.

Sakeena and Zaghloul were on the second floor. They heard the sound of the outer door near the Hagg's room being opened and shut: he had come back from his outing. They hurried down into the courtyard, and Zaghloul rushed outside to bring the two boys, and they went on tiptoe into their room.

One night Sakeena was woken by a voice in the courtyard. It was the Hagg calling out, "Anyone there?"

"Coming," she called back.

Zaghloul woke up to her voice. He dashed out, quickly rinsed his face to wake himself up, and entered the small corridor leading to the living room, beyond which lay the Hagg's room. He saw him sitting cross-legged on the bed.

"Zaghloul?" he said breathlessly.

"Yes."

"I forgot your name—sit with me for a while."

Zaghloul dragged the chair up to the bedside and sat down. The Hagg was breathing heavily and pressing his hand against his chest. Zaghloul regarded him sympathetically and asked, "Shall I make you an aniseed drink?"

The Hagg agreed with a nod of his head.

Zaghloul went out and found Sakeena standing at the entrance to the living room.

"Everything all right?"

"Make some aniseed."

He returned to the chair, muttering as if whispering to himself, "A touch of cold."

The Hagg's breathing calmed down. He asked him what

he had been saying. Zaghloul was surprised he had heard him.

"A touch of cold," he said

"That's right—a touch of cold."

He was still catching his breath with difficulty. He drank the aniseed and asked him about his work, though he did not seem to be interested to hear the answer. He moved his head backward and forward in a slow rhythm.

Zaghloul told him that he was working at the café on the river.

"I know it. They're all sons of bitches there."

He gave a long sigh, covering his eyes, and asked him if he had seen her.

"Who?"

"The Hagga."

Zaghloul regarded him with bulging eyes. Who could the Hagga be other than the late wife?

With a shudder running down his legs he whispered that he had not seen her.

Zaghloul had had enough—any talk about ghosts scared him. He could sense them almost touching him, and always at night he avoided places where he had heard that creatures appeared that you could not see.

The Hagg, leaning back, said that she did not like to come to him unless he was just about to go to sleep. "When she sees me sleeping she doesn't wake me up, but often she stands beside me for hours on end while I sleep." He was quiet, his eyes wandering.

He said that she was not comfortable either, being upset that she had left him.

"She asks me, 'Who'll stay by you if you're not well?' I

don't reply. I hear her and don't reply. What would I say to her?

"Even before she died, she would stay on in the room beside me, squeezing my arm until I went to sleep. Then she'd go to her room, and at times during the night I would be asleep and sense her walking on tiptoe, adjusting the cover around me and shutting any of the windows that might be open. She'd lean over me and I'd smell her breath and the scent of her hair, as she rested her face for a while against my shoulder, before going off. And then somebody said she was choleric, somebody in your café said that, and I heard about it. I tried to find out who it was, but I couldn't. Her face was a bit pale, and so they said she was choleric. They knew nothing about her. Even her own children didn't know. I was the only one who knew about her pains, and she told me not to tell the children—and I didn't."

He lay on his side with his back to the room. "Cover me," he said.

Zaghloul pulled the cover over him, and he went on. "She had her pains and she didn't complain. She said, 'I'm going before you, ya Hashem.' I look at her silently. What could I say to her? She sat on the chair—just where you are—and she said, 'I'm going, Hashem.' And she went."

Zaghloul stood there, his hand shivering on the arm of the chair. He looked at the back of the man as he lay there, his full body filling the bed, with the rattle of his breathing and the semi-darkness of the room. He wanted to reach the door without making a sound, and he heard the man saying, "Sit down a while, ya Zaghloul, until I go to sleep."

He said that if she saw him in the room she would not

come in, and he would have fallen sleep. "She doesn't like to visit me when there are other people with me."

He took long breaths, and the rattling increased. Talking tired him, but he did not want to stop.

He said that she always came, every day, and that her presence made things easier for him. She asked him, "Are you hiding anything from me, ya Hashem?"

"What would I have to hide from her? She never speaks frankly. She asks as though she's not asking. And she goes on to another topic. And all the time I'm thinking about what I could have hidden from her. And she asks me what I'm thinking about. I don't reply. One day, she asked me to pay her debt so that she could go up to heaven. Debt? What debt? I didn't know she was in debt to anyone. This time she spoke out: it was the rest of the account to Umm Saad—three and a half pounds. She said she was torn— she wanted to go up and didn't want to: if she went up, she wouldn't be able to come and see me, but she had grown tired of waiting, she wanted to rest, and most of her women friends had gone up. 'You don't know, ya Hashem, what I'm suffering.' And I wanted to tell her that I did know, but I didn't say anything. She pleaded with me to pay off her debt. I didn't know who Umm Saad was. I asked the two girls but they didn't know, and no one around here knew. Only today someone informed me that there was only one Umm Saad in the whole village, and she died ages ago. She used to sell spices and henna. I asked myself what account there could be between the Hagga and her—all the house needed in the way of spices was bought from the grocer by the two girls. Then I remembered: days before she went, she dyed her hands and feet with henna, and on that day

I was surprised because she hadn't used it since we were married. She was delighted with the coloring, spreading out her hands in front of me and saying, 'Have a look.'

"It was the henna, and we have to search for Umm Saad's heirs and pay them the debt. I'm worried that she doesn't have any heirs. If you could just help us, ya Zaghloul. Ask after them, and pay off the debt to them."

"First thing in the morning, ya Hagg, I'll start asking around."

"Good."

He turned over on his back, his troubled eyes wandering here and there. Then he closed them.

As Zaghloul stood there, he became aware that he was in his underclothes: his drawers and the torn undershirt. In his haste he had forgotten to pick up his gallabiya. He wanted to call his wife to bring it to him. But where was she now? She had left him and gone off.

The Hagg mumbled in a low voice, "Yes, I'm here."

He raised himself on his elbow and turned to Zaghloul. He was trembling violently and pointing with his hand. Zaghloul looked across to where he was pointing: a carafe of water with a glass alongside it on the small side table. He filled the glass and walked back to the bed, throwing glances around him. His extended hand trembled, and there was a trembling in his mouth too. Zaghloul pressed the glass into the crooked fingers. They shook violently and some of the water spilled out. He was unable to bring it up to his mouth and it would have fallen, but Zaghloul caught it. He raised the Hagg's head and brought the glass close up to his mouth. He took a sip, bringing his lips close together to stop the water leaking out, while his head fell back on the pillow. The water flowed out from the corner of his mouth, forming a small patch of wet on the pillow. His eyes were staring at the door.

"Ah, the henna on your hand . . . ,' he muttered breathlessly.

Zaghloul leaped backward, and in doing so knocked over the chair. As he made a dash for the door, he sensed that someone was passing close by him like a gust of wind. He screamed, and his feet seemed to cling to the ground. He caught sight of the Hagg's head rising up slightly and staring toward him before falling back onto the pillow.

Sakeena came at a run, with the two boys behind her. She enfolded Zaghloul, who shuddered in her embrace, and walked him to their room. She wanted to give him a glass of water, but he refused it with a motion of his hand. She did not stay with him until he had completely calmed down, but went to the Hagg's room.

She was away for a while and when she returned he looked at her inquiringly. "God's mercy on him," she said.

They went on sitting there in silence, and the two boys went back to sleep.

The first flickerings of dawn lit up the stairway.

"I'll just hop off to the girls."

"I'll go."

Sakeena thought and said, "We'd better have a bite to eat before we go out." And she woke the two boys.

The Son

Sakeena was sitting in her place on the stone bench and the two boys were where they usually sat. The young one had his head on her thigh, his skinny body stretched out, as he tried to get back to sleep. He had returned home with wounds on his legs and would not talk about it. She discovered them by chance: some of them were swollen with pus. She squeezed them to clear them, then bandaged them.

The older one squatted by the door not looking at her. Day does not break before she is off in her search of a couple of loaves of bread. The women in the houses do not leave their beds before the sun is up, the men having gone out early, to their jobs. Unlike the rest of them, her husband sat on the edge of the stone bench, a piece of straw in his mouth: he took it from the bedding before he got up, turning over the straw under him until he found a stalk he fancied. He did not tidy the bed afterward.

For a whole month, give or take a couple of days, he kept sitting in the same place, going out at sunset and coming back at midnight after everyone had gone home. She could sense him looking around for something to eat. Usually there would be a loaf she had borrowed during the day. Despite her warnings, the two boys took the opportunity of his absence from the house for any reason to bring down the suspended reed crate and take two or three loaves, leaving only one for their father, telling her as she threw stones at them, "One's enough for him—it's not as if he's been working."

The last time he had worked was in the café on the river. In those days she said, "Fair enough."

They cursed his mother and he kept quiet, and the second time it happened he kept quiet, but on the third occasion he cursed them back, and they rained down blows on him. Even the café owner joined in with them and threw him outside the area where the chairs were. His injuries were many, but the first thing he said when he came home was, "But the gallabiya's not damaged—not a tear in it."

As she sat there she cast a look at the big house and felt nostalgic for those days. There it is, closed up and silent as a ruin. And who looked after it? Its front was all spattered with dirt, and the waste space round it was filled with everything the wind had thrown there. When he saw her looking intently at the house, her younger son said, "Why are you upset? Isn't it enough that we had a few good days there? Perhaps there'll be another house." He sometimes surprised her with his words, and she did not know where he got them from.

This time Zaghloul stayed home for a long time, during which she borrowed bread three times from everybody she knew in the lane. She had not paid back the debt yet, and she was afraid that if she went to them a fourth time they would see that the debt had grown so big that she would be unable to pay it back; then they would think up excuses that she would find painful to hear. Perhaps if she sent the older boy to Abbas's oven? Government bread. So what, he had brought it twice before.

"Oh well, it tastes of bread—if only he can get some."

They called it government bread when they saw the police station in the village and the surrounding villages sending their trucks to the oven to buy large quantities of it for the soldiers and the prisoners.

Her eyes were on Zahir. He was leaning over and blowing into his hands made into fists between his knees. He stopped blowing and turned to her.

He crawled along until he reached the end of the stone bench, then brushed down his gallabiya and went off. "He understood without me saying anything to him."

Abbas's oven—when had he discovered it? He had passed by it without noticing it. It was the smell of the bread: it was still early, and he smelled the aroma, strong and penetrating, and turned to see the loaves of bread coming out right now from the oven, then being laid out on wooden tables at the entrance for people to take. The loaves were inflated, the surface slightly browned, and with little hollows where it had been burnt: these were small bubbles that had made their appearance as the loaf began to swell up, and where the flames got at them. He had seen it more than once when he used to crouch near the opening of the oven alongside his mother in the days when she used to bake her own bread. Usually the surface of the loaf would be brittle, and a mouthful of it would quickly melt in his mouth.

He stood staring at the slightly dark entrance. He noticed a corner table with a heap of scraps of bread, left over from the baking. He saw it as he approached, and it occurred to him that he should take some, and that the owner of the oven would not refuse him these loaves that were twisted or that had burst on the side. There were many pieces, loaves that had fallen when they were being taken out of the oven or being carried to the tables. He stretched out his hand and took a piece. A voice came to him from inside the darkness. "Take some if you want."

The oven had been turned off and Abduh the baker—he learned his name later—was removing the bits of wood that had been scattered in front of the oven with a long broom. "Come and sweep up the oven, and then you can fill your lap."

Zahir went in and was surprised by the man he had not seen before: short and with a curved back. The fire had licked at his arm and the side of his neck and his earlobe, leaving dead flesh. He stood in front of the mouth of the fire in long trousers and a vest. He had taken off his galla-biya when he gave the broom to Zahir, and now he seated himself at the entrance to smoke a cigarette.

Zahir finished quickly and stood waiting by the table with the scraps of bread. Abduh the baker looked at him and said, "Take as much as you can."

And he stood up to help him. Zahir opened up the lap of his gallabiya and the man scooped bread in with both hands several times.

"That's plenty," said Zahir, "It's absolutely full."

Unable to close up his lap, he hurried off outside. It was the first time he had taken bread home. It had been a day and a half since they had eaten anything. And his mother? What would she say when he came back with a lapful of bread?

They were sitting in their usual place on the stone bench. He stood in front of them, panting. Then he suddenly opened the gallabiya; his mother cried out and jumped up, dragging him by the shoulder inside the house, while his father and brother followed.

His mother brought down the reed crate and emptied what he was carrying into it.

"All that . . . all that . . . where did you get it?"

"From Abbas's oven."

"Abbas's oven? He was happy to give it to you?"

"Abduh the baker was there. He said, 'Sweep the oven and fill your lap.'"

"And you swept it?"

"Yes, with the long broom."

She took a bite from the bread, and they all stood staring at her and waiting for her to say something.

"By the Prophet, it tastes good."

His father did not say a word, though his face showed that he was happy about it. His mother brought out a couple of onions that she had been hiding for the day when there was cooking to be done. His father broke them open in the palms of his hands and hung them in a ring around the reed crate. On that day they ate their fill. There was a little left over in the crate, and he was content to hide his pride as he saw his bread hung up to the ceiling. On the same day, his father put on his gallabiya and went out. His mother followed him with her gaze and said, "May the Lord guide him and open things up before him." That day he worked with the carpenter who made waterwheels.

Zahir told his friend Abdullah when they were walking along the river bank, "Abduh the baker's a real lark, full of stories. Maybe I'll take you to the oven and you can hear for yourself."

"What stories?"

"I'll tell you."

And Zahir began telling the man's story.

"He said he'd come to the village two years ago. He'd seen many countries but never stayed in one place more than three or four years, and then he'd get fed up. I asked him, 'Fed up with the place, or with its people?'

"'Neither with the place nor the people: they're all more or less the same wherever you go. I'd just want to leave, and that was that.'

"He would work through the night and sleep when the sun came up. He'd sit close by the fire and gaze at it through the mouth of the oven and see the tongues of flame as they danced about and came to rest. They were friends, him and the fire."

"Have you ever heard anything like that?"

"Him and the fire?"

"Yes, the two of them."

"He was comfortable with the fire, and the fire with him. When it hissed, he would turn to it and would find that it was complaining about a piece of root that was thick and damp and refusing to burn, letting out thick smoke that stifled the flames. He'd stretch out his iron rod and drag away the piece of the blackened root, and the fire would quieten down, and its flames would start dancing about again, and it would sing its crackling song.

"Yes, he says extraordinary things, he says that the fire sings, and I ask him, 'Have you got any children, Uncle Abduh?'·

"'And what woman would have a man the fire had eaten part of?'

"All night long it was just him and the fire. He'd leave it to go to the bathroom and come back to find it as it was. 'And when it feels sleepy, when it's tired and wants to have a rest'—Uncle Abduh laughs—'the flames calm down a little, then disappear. The live coals are ablaze, and it looks beautiful.' Uncle Abduh laughs again. 'It's been feeling sleepy for a long time, then it goes out—and there's a small puff of smoke as it yawns, and I'm alongside it waiting for that yawn , and I stretch out beside it and go to sleep too.' And Uncle Abduh laughs and asks me if I think he's insane.

"And I say, 'What, Uncle Abduh? What's insane?'

"I don't understand a thing—I know what he's saying, but I don't understand.

"And then there was one night when he neglected the fire. He pushed a piece of root into the oven that was damp. He'd put it to one side for it to dry out, but he forgot about it and shoved it into the oven and turned his back on it. He heard the fire give a roar behind him, but he didn't look around as he was busy shouting at the baker, who'd brought the dough before it was ready. The argument between them went on for a long time. He felt the dense smoke inundating him, and he turned around and quickly pulled the piece of wood out from the oven. Then he thrust lots of pieces of dry wood into it, and turned back to the baker. A few moments later he heard the hissing and, as he turned, he was faced suddenly with a great wave of fire spurting out from the mouth of the oven. He didn't have the time to move away or lean sideways to pick up the bucket of water that was close at hand. The fire scorched him here and here, then when it had had its fill it retreated, and the flames calmed down. He just lay there staring at it, scarcely feeling what had happened to him. And Uncle Abduh laughs: it got angry, because he neglected it.

"And what am I supposed to say when he tells me these things? I look at him and I'm speechless.

"He told me I could come and take the scraps of bread every four days—the other days were booked. Before that he used to give it to a woman to feed her poultry. She offered to bring him three boiled eggs every day, but he told her he didn't eat them. Then another woman came along and asked him to give her some of it for her children. She had four children, and her husband worked for a couple of days and then was ill for a couple of days. He worked for a daily rate in the fields, she told him. She didn't complain or bewail her lot. She just said what she had to say, and that was it. He used to get a pain in his side after a few days of work and would scream and twist about. She took him to Salmawi the hospital attendant to give him injections, as well as drops for his eyes.

"He knows what he's doing—they all go to him. He saw her husband and said he had a kidney stone, and there was nothing for it but to have an operation at the government hospital. Her husband refused and said he'd never heard of anyone going in there and coming out on his own two feet. The hospital attendant—after all he worked there—got angry at this and shouted at him, 'How can you say that? Isn't it enough that you pay fifty piasters and go in and sleep on a bed and they take the stone out of you? The doctors there are the best in the world.'

"The attendant stopped, then said the man should make sure to have a few piasters with him, because the medicines, the gauze, and the cotton wool that were needed after the operation were all on his account. The hospital no longer had everything that was necessary. 'And the food has to be brought to you by your wife. But there's a solution. The patients there collect money among themselves, each according to his ability—to cover the price of the medicines and other things a new patient needs when they see he's penniless.'

"But her husband didn't want it.

"'I'll manage.'

"Abduh gave her bread for two days, and what's left over was enough for a third day, so she didn't come. He stopped giving bread to the woman with the eggs. Another woman came for the bread, who also had children. She would take bread for one day and she'd have enough for the next day. The wife of the sick man did him a good turn. She saw him one day washing his gallabiya behind the oven, and said she was angry he hadn't asked her to wash his clothes, and he should give them to her, as she had soap. He only had a few clothes. So he pointed to a small box of rusted tin above the oven. 'They're all there.'

"And boys come along: three or four, from one day to another. They stand in front of the table and eat. Munching away, they look at him, expecting him to drive them away each time.

"He talks and talks. If only you could see him when he's talking. I'm sitting squat-legged in front of him, and he sort of sees me and doesn't see me, and he doesn't ask himself whether the boy he has sat down to talk to hears or understands. He digs at the ground with his fingernail, looking here and there. The story I enjoyed most was the one about himself and the fire. I'd never heard about someone making friends with fire before. Thirty years, he says, he's been with the fire—he knows its moods and it knows his.

"He says he's thinking of leaving the village, and he's not been here two years yet. The people are fine, but the owner of the oven, Master Abbas—every day there's shouting and bellowing because he doesn't sell the scraps of bread, and his voice can be heard from one end of the lane to the other: 'Lots of people in the village want them! There's a demand for them and they have their price!'

"He knows it's not easy to find another baker in the place, or else he'd have got rid of him. Abduh lets him scream away and doesn't say a thing. But he can't take it any more. The other day, he pushed him in the chest, and his face was trembling with rage. 'You here, you're working at my place, so just listen to what I have to say!'"

Zahir sat there on the stone bench. He was tired of sitting and waiting for the day to start. Perhaps his mother would go out and come back empty-handed. He got to his feet, sensing their eyes watching him, but there was nothing he could do: he could not go to the oven every day. He would not find a single scrap of bread, it would have been taken by one of the two women.

He walked off.

He picked up a stone to throw at the dog that always lay in wait for him halfway along the lane, stretching its head out from a side alleyway and digging at the ground with its front claws as it prepared to attack. The stone hit it on the back and it gave a yelp and disappeared down the alleyway.

Zahir thought about calling on two or three of his friends, but it was early and they might still be asleep. Abdullah would be the only one to be up now, though his mother did not let him go out before having his breakfast. He had gone with him twice when his mother sent him to buy stewed beans, and one time he had bought some fried bean patties too. Abdullah had opened the paper cornet containing the patties and taken two out, eating one of them and offering the other one to Zahir, who, despite feeling extremely hungry, refused the patty, his mother having warned him and his brother not to take anything from anybody. But Abdullah had insisted, at which Zahir had said, "And what about your mother?"

"I'll say I ate them both."

He was the one friend he was seldom separated from. He had gone to Zahir's house on two occasions, and had sat with them on the stone bench. He had no doubt heard that his mother borrowed bread. Some of the children used to shame him with that when they were quarreling.

One day Abdullah said to him, "Listen, I've got an idea— wait for me behind the house and I'll lower something down to you from up above on the roof."

"What thing?"

"You'll see, but don't make a sound."

It looked liked a new game Abdullah was playing—
wanting, as usual, to surprise him with it. So he waited
behind the house, keeping close in to the wall.

He heard a "Ssh!" and saw Abdullah sprawled out on the
roof with his head thrust out, looking in both directions.
The string was let down, its end twisted around a loaf of
bread, a large, dry loaf that swung as it was lowered. Zahir
stared at it, his hands at the ready to catch it if it fell. He
undid the string and looked at Abdullah, who was signing
to him to hurry away. Zahir rushed off with the loaf and
stood waiting for him at the top of the lane, but he did not
come. He looked around for a quiet place where he could
pause to eat the loaf without being disturbed. He placed
the loaf in his lap and raised his knees to hide it. He slowly
chewed the first mouthful, enjoying the way the edge of it
melted stickily on his tongue, as a gurgling sound came in
protest from his empty stomach.

The loaf calmed the sting of hunger a little and allowed
him to make an unhurried tour of the fruit and vegetable
shops, picking up the pieces that had rotted and fallen not
far from the crates. He threw away the part that was bad
and ate the rest. More than once a woman selling the produce held out an undamaged cucumber or tomato to him,
even though he was moving on.

Time after time he found himself waiting for a loaf from
Abdullah. If he began by eating the bread before anything
else, his stomach would not be upset, but if he started off
with the vegetables and fruit, his stomach would churn
around with gurgling noises.

They were often together when Abdullah went home at
noon, the time for his lunch. At first he was surprised that

there were people who had set times for eating, but he did not ask about this, as he did not like to ask about things he did not understand: he preferred to wait until the information came by itself. As they were walking along, Abdullah would say he would be letting down the string. Before, he used to protest; now when he heard this, the refusal was on his tongue, but he said nothing. Abdullah's father was a teacher at the compulsory school, and Abdullah possessed no less than four changes of gallabiya, and wore an undervest, and ate three meals a day. He never talked about what he ate, though Zahir would have liked to hear about it.

One day he was surprised to find that the loaf that was lowered was broken on one side, and when he took hold of it he found a number of pieces of stuffed cabbage inside it. He gazed at them in joy. He had eaten them three times before, once at home a long time ago, and twice in the house of Hagg Hashem. The time at home, he and his brother had sat beside their mother from the beginning of the process. She had pulled off the cabbage leaves to stuff them, and had cut the stalks and head into small pieces and salted them with water in a large jar. She did not throw away a single part of the cabbage. They did not wait for the cabbage to pickle, and finished off what was in the jar the very same day, leaving nothing but the salty water. She chased them about in the courtyard. They tried to help her in rolling the leaves to make the stuffed cabbage, but she scolded them and chased them away. From time to time she looked up at them, her face beaming with pleasure.

"That's it," she said, "I've nearly finished."

They could not wait for the stuffed cabbage to be properly cooked. They pleaded with her until she took out a couple of pieces each. "How can you eat it when it's not done yet?"

If only she had known that he was now eating nearly a whole loaf every day, and sometimes with stuffed cabbage. He did not tell her, and he could not take it to them. She would have plenty to say, and he would have nothing to say in return. And anyway, what would they take but a fragment of bread each?

Many times Abdullah would surprise him, when they were wandering about in the evening, with a small scrap of paper wrapped around a kidney or some chicken gizzards, and once a rabbit's head and part of its neck. He would keep the package in his pocket, and Abdullah would ask him why he did not eat it, and he would say, "Later on."

He himself did not know why he did not eat it in front of him. He would touch the package in his pocket from time to time, and as soon as they parted he would take it out and eat it.

Their walk would begin when they met up to go to the fields, one of them putting his arm around the other's shoulder. They would look for mulberry and sycomore fig trees tucked far away from the much-frequented paths, and always found the branches heavy with fruit. Then they would go fishing. They kept their hooks and their lengths of cane on the bank of a side water channel. Their catch consisted of small fish, which they threw back when it was time to leave. After that they went to the river. The first time Abdullah went into the water he was frightened; he clung onto the bank and splashed his feet about. After Zahir had taught him to swim, they went out into the middle of the river, sometimes right to the other shore and surprised the train passengers by appearing naked and running along beside the train, as the passengers hurled insults at them.

When the time came for Abdullah's lunch, and they were on their way back, Abdullah often complained about his father, saying that he stopped him doing all the things he loved: going to the fields, swimming in the river, and fishing. His father saw bilharzia and stomach worms everywhere and always warned him against them. "For the smallest thing he beats me. If he sees me barefoot in the house he gives me a slap. If he's talking to me and I happen to turn away for any reason, there's another slap. If I raise my voice or if I cry because he's hit me and I don't understand why, he beats me again so I won't cry."

He would slip into the house to wash his feet and put on slippers before meeting his father. Zahir listened, but found nothing to say.

They kept quiet about their walking tours, even from their friends.

One day Abdullah asked him, "Why don't you go to school like the others?"

"That's just how it is."

"No, tell me why."

"If anybody had told me to go to school, I wouldn't have said No."

"I don't understand."

"Nor me."

Abdullah said he was asking because his father had asked him the same question. He asked him about his friends, one by one, and what they did when they played games. "And when it came to your name, he asked me why you didn't go to school. And I said I didn't know.

"He said, 'Have you asked him?'

"'No.'

"'And his father, what does he do?'

"I said all I knew was that he sometimes works in cafés.

"'And apart from cafés?'

"'How do I know?' And he gave me a slap. I should have asked you and found out and told him politely. Sometimes I burst out shrieking and crying and stamping on the ground, and he falls on me with blows, and my mother comes along at my screaming and pulls me from his hands. She asked me, 'And have you been to their house?'

"I said I hadn't.

"And in the end he said, 'Don't go out with him from now on, and don't have him as a friend.'

"'All right,' I say.

"Who'll tell him we go out together? And even if he knows, it's just a slap in the face. So what? I'm used to it and it doesn't scare me."

Zahir became careful about going around with Abdullah. He would accompany him to the nearest lane to his house and then go his way. They avoided the main streets, where his father might be walking. And when he went to call him he hid at the corner of the lane watching for his father to leave the house, knowing the times he went out and came home. He would see him going out, tall and thin, and gathering his gallabiya up around his body when he came near any dogs, fearful of being soiled. As soon as had he gone some distance, Zahir would give a whistle, and Abdullah would come out to him. Sometimes his father would have asked his mother not to let him go out, as a punishment, so in answer to the whistle Abdullah would appear on the roof and lie down flat, and Zahir would stick close to the wall, and they would exchange words in a low voice. He would tell him what he and his friends had done and where they had gone, and Abdullah would stifle his laughs and shake his legs and ask, "And tonight?"

"I don't know—perhaps we'll just sit around and tell stories."

"You can tell me tomorrow."

"So when are you going out?"

"In a couple of days. Wait, I'll lower you down a loaf and a bit of cheese."

At times, Abdullah would get into fights with his friends, coming to blows with them. Being delicately built, he was not good at scrapping. The boys would abuse him about his father as a usurer. Zahir did not understand the meaning of what they were saying and he did not ask Abdullah about it, although he realized it was some sort of insult. He would see him rushing off to do battle, and one of the boys would quickly have him on the ground, at which Zahir would come forward and grab the boy by the throat, and the others would retreat, knowing Zahir's strength and courage. His punches were directed rapidly to the face, and the blood soon flowed from someone's nose or mouth. Then in a flash Zahir would disappear.

One day he was snooping around Abdullah's house. It was noon and his father should have left, but he was not sure. He waited for what he thought was sufficient time and then gave his whistle. After a while he spotted Abdullah on the roof with what looked like a paper airplane in his hand. He motioned to him to come closer, and so

Zahir did. Abdullah lay flat on his stomach, his head over the edge of the roof. Raising the airplane in his hand, he said, "It's missing the tail. I'll do it today. See?"

"Beautiful. Are you going to fly it on the roof?"

"There's no wind on the roof. It needs fields and the riverbank."

"Yes, you're right. When you come out we'll fly it there."

He saw a change come over Abdullah's face, and his body cowered and moved back. At the same moment he became aware of the sound of light footsteps behind him, and turned to find Abdullah's father close by. Zahir prepared to take to flight, but the man signaled to him to stay where he was. Zahir was rooted to the spot. Abdullah's father gazed at him for a moment, then gathered up his gallabiya so it would not touch the ground.

"So you're Zahir?"

Zahir nodded in silence.

"Come here." Zahir walked forward until he was standing in front of him. Abdullah's father stretched out his hand and seized him by the shoulder. Zahir could feel his fingers boring painfully into his flesh.

"I don't know why the Lord afflicted us with you people. Is there no one but my son? You've got all the kids in the world, so what brings you to my house? What should I do with you? Answer me."

He shook him violently, as Zahir stared into his face and said nothing. The face was thin, with protruding bones and an overall pallor, and a slight trembling of the mouth.

"I'm telling you to answer me."

His voice rose until it was a shout. The neighbors gathered at the head of the lane. They just stood there, no one advancing or uttering a word. The pain in his shoulder was growing worse: the fingers squeezing into his flesh were pressing down on the bone. He leaned forward slightly, wishing to ease the man's grip. He was given a slap and stood gazing down at the ground.

"Look at me. This lane, from one end to the other, and the lane next to it, and the one after that: if I see you in any one of them I'll break your neck."

Zahir tried to move slightly away from the man's breath, which was searing his face. He dragged him by the shoulder of his gallabiya. The cloth was not strong enough, and a large tear appeared, baring Zahir's naked shoulder.

"What's this?" said the man, looking at him in surprise.

He suddenly quietened down and turned to the people standing at the head of the lane. "Tell them in the house to bring a gallabiya from the clothes of the dog on the roof."

Zahir took a quick look at the roof and spotted Abdullah, who was still sprawled out, wiping his eyes with his fist.

The gallabiya was quickly produced and the father threw it across Zahir's shoulder. "Take this in place of the rag you're wearing."

He took two paces back and shook out his gallabiya. He was ready to go back into the house when Zahir threw the gallabiya to the ground and walked away. The man's voice followed him. "Look at the son of a bitch."

Sakeena was at her place on the stone bench awaiting the coming of day, which was drawing near. The sun appeared on the horizon, its rays touching the tip of the minaret of the mosque. The dew on the dust of the lane began to dry off, and the sound of coughing came from here and there. Stretching out her legs, she began rubbing her knee. "Nearly there. I'll check on them soon."

Raising his head from her thigh, Ragab looked around him. Zaghloul, at the other end of the stone bench, was sucking the length of straw and watching a dog sniffing the side of the wall, while Zahir squatted by the door not looking at his mother. He was afraid she would ask him to go to Abbas's oven. Abduh the baker had left two days ago — he had seen him carrying his box on his way to the station, and Abduh had waited until he caught up with him.

"So, Zahir, the time has come."

Zahir said nothing, and Abduh the baker was silent.

Modern Arabic Literature

The American University in Cairo Press is the world's leading publisher of Arabic literature in translation.

For a full list of available titles, please go to:

mal.aucpress.com